Previously published Worldwide Mystery title by
JOYCE CATO

BIRTHDAYS CAN BE MURDER

JOYCE CATO

AN INVISIBLE
Murder

WORLDWIDE®

TORONTO • NEW YORK • LONDON
AMSTERDAM • PARIS • SYDNEY • HAMBURG
STOCKHOLM • ATHENS • TOKYO • MILAN
MADRID • WARSAW • BUDAPEST • AUCKLAND

Recycling programs
for this product may
not exist in your area.

An Invisible Murder

A Worldwide Mystery/October 2014

First published by Robert Hale Limited

ISBN-13: 978-0-373-26917-4

Copyright © 2012 by Joyce Cato

Printed in U.S.A.

PROLOGUE

THE JEWELLED DAGGER glinted in a shaft of bright June sunlight, its shadow as black as death against the wall on which it was hung.

It was a strange-looking piece. The handle was thick and curved, designed to fit snugly in the hand, and was richly encrusted with rubies, emeralds, pearls and sapphires. In contrast, the blade was as straight as a die, long, narrow and almost rounded, but coming to a wickedly sharp point. It looked more like a stiletto that some nineteenth-century Italian nobleman might once have carried for his personal protection, than the patently older and authentically Indian weapon that it actually was.

Suddenly, the sparkle of its gems was dimmed as a shadow fell across it, and thoughtful eyes studied it minutely. The killer looked at the dagger for a long, long while, planning just how, where and when to use it.

Finally satisfied, the killer nodded and moved away and once more the Indian dagger basked in the light, its gems sending shafts of lively colour across the ancient walls.

ONE

THE ANCIENT, bright cherry-red van whined like a wasp as it buzzed up the country road leading to the small Oxfordshire market town of Bicester. Although it was the first week of June, it was unseasonably cold, and its driver was wearing a warm outfit and gloves. Miss Jenny Starling, travelling cook and one-woman crusader for real food was constantly on the alert against colds. Her profession and sneezing and coughing were not exactly compatible.

The turn off to the small village of Upper Caulcott, where Jenny was headed, suddenly appeared and she indicated right, keeping a wary lookout for any road signs that might lead her to Avonsleigh Castle. As she drove, she wondered what her best approach would be for the important interview that lay ahead.

She had seen the advertisement for a cook/chef at Avonsleigh Castle in the *Oxford Times* just last week, and had promptly applied for it, enclosing her full curriculum vitae, plus a pile of impressive references, and had not been surprised to be summoned for interview. But she had never so much as set foot in a genuine lord's pad before.

She sighed deeply and tried not to anticipate. She would play the interview by ear, as she had always done in the past.

Jenny soon found herself entering a small but attractive village where a Victorian coronation oak spread splendid branches over the village pub and she stopped to ask an old man walking his dog the way to Avonsleigh.

'The castle's just up ahead on the hill,' the old man said, pointing his walking stick in the general direction. 'Follow the bend around, and you'll be bound to see it. Bugger's big enough,' he stated amiably, and grinned at her.

Jenny grinned back and set off, and soon found herself at her destination. The bulk of Avonsleigh Castle had been built just after the civil war, and looked more like a really large manor house than anything else, but it did have a few turrets and a dry moat to boast of.

As the van reached a tiny wooden drawbridge and crossed it, the air echoed to the empty clang of iron and wood as they went over, and she pulled the van to a stop in a small quad. There, she withdrew her six-foot, Junoesque frame from the van with unconscious grace, and took off her white knitted hat, revealing a lush, shoulder-length bob of thick, dark brown hair.

To the east were the stables which, she saw to her disappointment, had been converted into a tea-room for the tourist visitors. To the west was the main entrance, gained through a double, iron-studded oak door that looked massive, heavy and ancient. Jenny knew better than to approach them, and looked around instead for a side entrance.

As she did so, a small wooden door set in the south-facing wall opened slowly, and a man emerged. At about five feet ten, he was dressed in a dark-blue suit and impeccable white shirt. Even from a distance, he was unmistakably a member of staff.

Jenny locked the van, then walked towards him, her clear and quite beautiful blue eyes assessing him as unobtrusively as his own gaze assessed her. When they were face to face, both had come to the conclusion that the other would do very well.

'Miss Starling?' the man murmured, and Jenny smiled and inclined her head and followed him into a small anteroom that was extremely cold, but at least well lit. Jenny fought back a shiver as he took her coat, and followed him out into the main hall, which was as impressive as anything she had ever seen. Traditional stone slabs stretched across the floor, whilst bulging and thick walls were painted a dazzling white. Standing guard were several suits of genuine armour, and hanging from a towering ceiling was a huge old-fashioned, candle-bedecked crystal chandelier that tinkled melodiously in the draught.

Jenny, wide-eyed, continued to follow the butler as he led the way past a sweeping, ornately carved wooden staircase. Lining the walls were landscape paintings, and Jenny noticed a woman, standing halfway up the stairs, studying one with intense interest. She had time to wonder briefly who the other woman might be, and then the butler was taking her down another cold passageway that seemed to twist and turn forever.

Eventually he reached a door and tapped discreetly, before ushering her inside. The contrast was almost overwhelming. From cold bare walls to a vast expanse of warm, carpeted, light-painted elegance was a bit of a shock to the system, but Jenny supposed she'd get used to it. If she was to work in a castle, she had better quickly become castle-oriented.

The room itself had windows that faced a stone-flagged terrace, which in turn gave way to lawns, interspersed with bushes, rose-beds and herbaceous borders. The view across to the village was awe-inspiring. The walls here were also crammed with paintings, there having been several avid art collectors in the Avonsleigh ancestry.

Jenny gave them a quick, appreciative glance, and then the butler coughed. 'Miss Starling, my lady,' he said simply and withdrew, leaving her alone with every sense snapped alert.

At first she thought that there was only one other person in the room, in the form of Lady Avonsleigh, Vivienne Margaret, who, she would quickly learn, was called simply Lady Vee by friends, family and staff alike. She sat on a sturdy French-looking sofa, dressed in English tweeds and very sensible, lace-up, walking shoes. She had obviously reached her sixties, and her hairdresser had insisted on a light blue rinse. Her heavy jowls gave her the look of an amiable bulldog. Her hands, however, were littered with rings encasing stones that would make even the most hardened of jewellers break out in a cold sweat.

At her feet, a filthy English Setter slumbered in grey-spotted bliss.

Lady Vee looked up at the same moment that Jenny looked down, and the two women instantly recognized the other. Not that they'd ever met before—they just simply and instantly knew what kind of person the other was, and was glad of it. Jenny knew there was a word for it—*simpatico* was it?—or something along these lines.

'Please sit down, Miss Starling,' Lady Vee said, her voice booming out like a foghorn. She'd probably become used to shouting in order for the servants to hear her through all these solid doors, Jenny thought tolerantly, and promptly sat down. Already she knew this interview was going to go well.

'George, ring Janice for some tea would you, there's a dear?' Lady Vee prompted, and it was only then that the cook noticed the man seated in a huge wing-backed chair placed at a comfortable right angle to a blazing fire.

As Jenny watched, the rake-thin man with a huge nose and fiercely blazing blue eyes reached forward and pulled on a bell rope hanging discreetly against one velvet, floor-length curtain. His lordship (who else could it be?) then leaned back. Throughout the entire procedure, he had not taken his eyes off the book he was reading. Like his wife, he was dressed in traditional countryman's clothes, and was wearing a particularly odoriferous pair of Wellington boots.

She turned back immediately to the boss. As imposing as his lordship undoubtedly was, Jenny was under no illusions as to who was the true master of Avonsleigh Castle.

'Well, I suppose we'd better make a start,' Lady Vee said briskly. 'I must say your references are particularly impressive, Miss Starling. You make a lasting impression on your employers, it seems,' she added, button-brown eyes definitely twinkling.

Jenny said modestly, 'I seem to. Yes.'

Just then the door opened and a very pretty, blonde-haired maid walked in, carrying an enormous tray on which sat a tea-pot covered with a cosy in a particularly garish design, a tall silver milk jug, obviously Georgian, with a matching sugar bowl and spoon. The cups and saucers, a delicate rosebud design, were Royal Doulton, or Jenny was a monkey's uncle. And Jenny Starling definitely was *not* a monkey's uncle.

All in all, it was a very revealing tray. Wealth sat side by side with English eccentricity in a way that immediately soothed the nerves and reassured her.

The maid transferred the whole assembly onto the table in a matter of seconds and withdrew. 'We'll let it brew, of course,' Lady Vee said, making Jenny fairly beam. Someone else who appreciated proper tea! Yes indeed, she thought, mentally hugging herself with joy, things were off to an auspicious start.

'Now, perhaps you could give us some idea of, say, an average meal. What would you cook for my husband and me, on a day like today?' Lady Vee abruptly came straight to the point. Jenny liked that. And the fact that she was conducting the interview herself bode well. Here was a person who took her food seriously. As she should.

Jenny looked out of the window at the cold day, remembered the chilly corridors and dismissed anything remotely to do with salad. She glanced back at the boss. You didn't get all those chins eating lettuce and tomato, she judged happily, and smiled. 'Well, your ladyship, I am basically a traditional cook. That is, I specialize in English cuisine.'

Out of the corner of her eye, and for the first time, she noticed the man of the house lower his book. No doubt he had attended Eton and then Oxford, and thus had been raised on spotted dick and custard. In Jenny's opinion, children never outgrew their favourites, and taking a deep breath, she leapt right in.

'I think a steak and onion pudding—made with real suet, mind—would go down well, so long as its steamed for a good three hours. And none of this modern microwave oven nonsense either,' she added, and paused to gauge her audience's reaction.

Over to her right, his lordship's book had lowered all the way to his lap now, and his wife's bright cheeks had become, if anything, even a little rosier. 'Vegetables, of course, depends on personal taste and the season, but good early broad beans, and spring cabbage, if seasoned right, are good sources of iron.' She noticed his lordship's hands tighten on his book and, sensing she was losing him, added quickly, 'And of course, potatoes must always be served. With a steamed steak pudding, I would serve them mashed, with plenty of milk and butter. And plenty of them. There's nothing so…unappealing…as…stingy potatoes,' Jenny said, suddenly and—potentially catastrophically—losing all her concentration.

It had never happened to her before, but on this occasion it could most definitely be forgiven. For, on the table in front of her, the teapot, in its brightly knitted cosy, was beginning to move slowly across the silver tray.

So she didn't see his lordship lick his chops with satisfaction, and totally missed the sigh of pure pleasure that Lady Vee gave over this recital of potato worship.

'And for pudding?' George, for the first time, actually spoke. He was leaning forward eagerly in his chair now.

Jenny, with some considerable effort, managed to drag her eyes away from the perambulating teapot and forced her mind back to the job in hand. But it took some doing. You expected teapots to stand still, after all.

'Well, now, if you've had a heavy main course, a lighter pudding is usually advisable,' she began. Then, realizing that she was about to lose him again, added hurriedly, 'But by that I don't mean any of these fancy, foreign puddings. No. Let me see—rhubarb should be just superb at this time of year. There's nothing like fresh rhubarb served with a good vanilla custard…after a…heavy dinner….' Jenny trailed off again, noticing that the tea cosy was picking up just a little bit of speed now. Not that it was exactly galloping across the tray mind. Just inexorably moving. And moving, moreover, in *her* direction.

Only by the greatest effort of will, did Jenny manage to remain sitting in her seat. Her eyes, however, became wider and rounder as the tea cosy ambled inexorably her way. Try as she might, she couldn't recall of ever having heard of a haunted teapot before. Haunted houses by the dozen, naturally. Haunted railway depots, no problem. There'd even been reports of a haunted shoe factory, once. But a possessed teapot?

She supposed that any self-respecting castle would have its own ghost, but she wished the phantom would make itself scarce, at least until she'd secured a position here. It was definitely putting her off her stride.

'And how would you cook the rhubarb?' Lady Vee asked, swallowing hard as she contemplated the thought of rhubarb and custard, steaming hot from the kitchens.

Once more, Jenny dragged her eyes from the moving tea cosy and concentrated on securing the job that she already knew, in her heart of hearts, was hers for the taking.

'Oh, no water, definitely not. Rhubarb reduces easily, and rhubarb juice should never be contaminated with water,' Jenny's voice was just a tad shaky. 'A touch of orange juice—pure, mind—is all it would need. And a certain amount of sugar of course.'

The boss was already nodding her head in undisguised glee. 'Yes, yes. I certainly agree.'

'And not too much sugar either,' the cook added. 'Custard, made with the cream off the top of the milk is all the contrast that's needed.'

'Used to eat raw rhubarb as a boy m'self,' George put in, unexpectedly. 'Old Smithers, the gardener, used to laugh himself sick over it.' And with that, he abruptly returned to his book once more.

The tea cosy was now only inches away from the edge of the tray, and thus, Jenny's lap. The gaudy blues, oranges and greens of the knitted horror were sending cold shivers up and down her spine.

'Do you have any specialities?' Lady Vee prompted eagerly. Either she hadn't noticed that her teapot was on walkabout, or she was so used to the castle's restless spooks that she now took no notice. Jenny only hoped that she could acquire some of her ladyship's *savoir-faire*. As it was, her hands were clenching and unclenching nervously in her lap, and her top lip was becoming…yes…was most definitely becoming moist.

'Er…well, bacon clanger springs to mind,' Jenny said desperately, her eyes glued to the tea cosy. It never slowed or stopped, but just kept up its ponderous, remorseless pace. It wouldn't be so bad if the spook moaned or rattled the odd chain or two. That at least might serve to break some of its fearsome attraction for her. With a huge effort, the cook looked back at her ladyship. 'Made with proper bacon—or even boiling bacon if you prefer, and of course, plenty of leeks. That's the secret of a good bacon clanger,' she gulped, hoping her voice wasn't as high-pitched as it sounded to her own ears.

'And for pudding?' George asked yet again, leaving Jenny in no doubt as to where his heart lay. It gave her fresh nerve, and she positively beamed at him. She did so approve of a man who liked his puddings.

'Oh, let's see. Jam roly-poly—but no, that's too much dough at one sitting. Any fruit crumble would be good. Or even a milky dish—rice pudding perhaps, or tapioca. Then there's treacle tart, or apples, cored and stuffed with mincemeat and baked in cider.…'

She turned back to the boss, deliberately keeping her gaze averted from the table. Any moment now the possessed pot would reach the edge, and then what would it do? Interview or not, if it leapt into her lap, Jenny thought she might very well scream the place down.

'Wonderful,' Lady Vee sighed, and then a look of doubt crossed her face.

But not even a haunted teapot could put Jenny Starling off her stroke when it came to the crunch, and the wily cook instantly guessed the cause of that troubled look and set out to remedy it. 'Of course, these traditional foods are all very well when cooking for the family, but they won't do when one is entertaining,' she carried on briskly. 'Naturally, when you have guests, I wouldn't dream of serving such dishes.'

She saw his lordship wilt, and the glum but resigned look that passed over the face of his wife. 'Of course, that doesn't mean you need to suffer,' Jenny added quickly. 'For instance, salmon en croute, with the pink flesh showing through a lattice of gold puff pastry and shaped like the fish itself looks splendid enough to satisfy any guest, but it tastes delicious. And then there's game. Very elegant, but also tasty and filling. Pigeon pie, pheasant under glass, quails cooked in aspic…er….'

The teapot had reached the edge of the tray, seemed to hesitate and then began moving back. Presumably the spook inside the porcelain had no head for heights.

'And puddings can be even better,' she continued, wondering if it would be considered a social gaffe to warn Lady Avonsleigh that a haunted teapot was headed her way. Perhaps etiquette demanded that one simply ignored that kind of thing? 'For instance white choco-

late and elderflower gateau looks very elegant and so-
phisticated, but tastes even better.'

Jenny turned back to Lord Avonsleigh who was
blinking rapidly, and no doubt trying to conjure up the
image of a white chocolate cake. Then his gaze fell to
the teapot, and his mouth dropped open.

'Good Gad!' he yelped. 'Poltergeists!'

His wife jumped at her husband's no-doubt unexpected and uncharacteristic display of liveliness,
glanced at the teapot and sighed. 'No dear. It must be
Henry again.'

'Oh,' his lordship subsided immediately and once
again rang the bell-rope, before picking up his ubiquitous book. He sighed deeply.

'When can you start, Miss Starling?' Lady Vee
asked, and Jenny, again with some effort, dragged her
thoughts away from Henry, and smiled. From her hosts'
reaction, obviously 'Henry' was a friendly ghost. Or
one who was, at least, not likely to start hurling the
furniture about.

'I have my suitcase with me, as it happens,' she replied. 'I could start right away,' she added simply. The
advertised post had included a 'live in' option.

Lady Vee beamed her pleasure, and didn't see the
need to comment on the truly amazing gall required to
come to an interview with her case already packed. Besides, having now met Jenny Starling it seemed somehow quite appropriate.

Just then the door opened, and the pretty blonde maid
returned. Lady Vee pointed at the tea cosy, still ambling,

and the maid sighed. 'I'm sorry m'lady. Henry does have this way with him....'

Her ladyship, not looking a bit put out, merely smiled.

Again, Jenny turned her thoughts to Henry. Obviously a well-known ghost, and not one to strike panic into the hearts of the castle's denizens. A young page perhaps, killed in some forgotten battle?

The maid walked to the table and unceremoniously plucked off the tea cosy revealing the tortoise that lurked underneath. The reptile raised its scrawny neck and gazed about in stolid, reptilian dignity.

Jenny just managed to stop herself from laughing hysterically out loud. 'A tortoise,' she said, and caught Lady Vee's questioning glance. Jenny forced her face into neutrality. 'I did just wonder...ghosts....' she murmured diffidently, waving one hand vaguely and casually in the air and letting her voice trail off gently.

Lady Vee, suddenly realizing that this wondrous cook had just sat through the entire interview in a state of fear and trepidation without so much as raising a single squawk, felt almost humble.

'Janice, ask Meecham to prepare the blue room for Miss Starling at once. She'll be staying,' she said simply.

And the two women beamed their mutual contentment at each other.

TWO

JENNY'S SUITCASE WAS in fact a heavy-weight nylon ruck-sack and, after she'd retrieved it from the back of her colourful van, allowed the butler to escort her to her room.

The blue room turned out to be just that. As Mee-cham, who'd insisted on taking the bag from her, set it down, Jenny found herself very glad that she happened to like the colour blue. If she hadn't, the room would have driven her insane in a matter of hours. For a long moment the statuesque cook stood in respectful silence by the bed. It was a full four-poster, complete with swathes of blue and gold material and intricately carved posts of a wood so dark it might have been ebony. In this room too, the walls were smothered with paintings.

'Would you like to unpack now, Miss Starling, or shall I take you to the kitchens?' Meecham enquired.

'Oh, the kitchens, please,' Jenny said at once. Her bedroom had a lovely view of the meadows that lay on the north side, but the kitchen was always where her heart was.

Meecham smiled in approval. The old cook had left last week and, like the rest of the staff, he'd hoped that a new cook would be appointed before she left, since everyone knew that the kitchen help would hardly prove to be an adequate stand-in.

'There are several members of staff besides myself who eat in.' He decided to start her education right away as he took her down stairs and corridors that would have made the maze at Hampton Court Palace seem like a doddle. 'As well as myself, there is my daughter, Gayle, who also acts as a guide at the castle—the family apartments are of course strictly private. Then there's Elsie Bingham, she's in charge of the kitchen work and the most important member of staff as far as you're concerned, I'm sure. Janice, the young lady who served your tea also eats her midday meal with us. She works in the tea-room in the afternoons. None of the gardening staff eats in, of course,' he added, just in case this competent-looking woman wasn't quite as experienced as she made out.

He turned after negotiating one particularly narrow twist, and saw a look of amused but friendly understanding on her face, and gave a small nod of satisfaction. Obviously his warning had been unnecessary.

'Then there's the teaching staff.'

'Teaching staff?' Jenny asked, wondering how much further it was to the kitchen, and feeling more and more relieved that it would be Meecham's job to serve the food.

'Yes, Lady Roberta is sixteen, and the only granddaughter of Lord and Lady Avonsleigh. They had two sons, but the elder and his wife were killed in a boating accident ten years ago. They had one daughter, Lady

Roberta. She is now sixteen, and being educated at the castle. Naturally.'

'Of course,' Jenny murmured, but was actually rather surprised. In this modern day and age, surely not many members of the British aristocracy were still taught at home by tutors?

'The youngest son and now heir is Sir Richard, but he's abroad at the moment. America,' Meecham paused. 'He is, I believe, bringing home a new bride in a few weeks' time.'

Jenny hoped the new arrival wouldn't feel too out of place here. It must be hard, uprooting to a totally new environment.

'Mr Powell-Brooks is primarily Lady Roberta's art teacher,' Meecham carried on. 'The Avonsleigh family has a long history of art appreciation, and for centuries all the Avonsleighs have been taught both theory and practice when it comes to fine art. It's a tradition that will, I'm sure, never be broken.'

Regardless of talent or aptitude, Jenny surmised wryly. Although she could imagine the poor old man upstairs being forced into art lessons as a child, she just couldn't see him producing anything more than a few pathetic daubs. Still, no doubt her ladyship, having married into the family, had been spared the ordeal.

She wondered how Lady Roberta was doing.

'Mr Powell-Brooks also takes some other lessons, standing in for…the governess…when appropriate.'

Jenny wondered if she'd imagined his slight hesitation when mentioning the governess, but just then he opened the door onto the most spectacular kitchen she'd ever seen.

And Jenny Starling had seen plenty.

It was the size, of course, that first struck her. Here, in the olden days, over twenty servants had worked and toiled together, butchering, baking huge amounts of coarse bread in vast ovens, and preparing meals for hundreds of people. The walls had been recently white-washed, and huge ovens proliferated. Real copper pots and pans hung from wooden pegs, contrasting oddly with the more modern appliances of dishwasher and microwave.

In spite of all this, Jenny was struck at once by the welcome warmth and homely feel of the place. There were several easy chairs scattered about and, in the centre of the room, a vast, spotlessly clean wooden table dominated its surroundings. It had a full complement of high-backed chairs and, sitting in one, drinking a cup of tea, was a woman who was probably in her forties, but looked older. Her hair was pulled back and her hands were thin and knobbly. She was, Jenny surmised, a woman who knew what hard work was all about—a real rarity in this push-button age.

Meecham coughed, and the older woman looked up. Her eyes fastened on the cook, a look of fear and hope curiously mixed in her dull grey eyes. Jenny understood it at once. A cook could make life hell for a co-worker, and she was anxious at once to reassure her. She was already moving forward with a kind but firm look on her face. 'Hello, you must be Elsie.' She held out her hand, and the older woman flushed and gave a brief handshake.

'I'm the new cook. Please call me Jenny. I'm sure we shall get along splendidly.'

Elsie glanced away, reserving judgement. Satisfied that she'd done as much as she could on a first meeting—only time would reassure her most important helper that all would be well—she turned back to Meecham. 'The ovens are all electric?'

Meecham nodded. 'We're not on the gas main here.'

Jenny was content. Although she could cook on anything, she preferred electric.

For the next half-hour she toured her domain, making mental inventories, approving of some of the older equipment whilst making mental notes to bring in a few new gadgets of her own.

'Well, Elsie, I think a cup of tea would be welcome about now,' she hinted gently at last, and her helper, without a word, set about the task. Just then the door opened and a young woman walked in. She could only be Gayle, Meecham's daughter, for she had her father's dark eyes and slightly supercilious face. Yet she also had a slender grace that probably made most men look twice. Her hair was pulled back, revealing a long, graceful neck. Nowhere near beautiful, and yet, in a way, very attractive.

'Gayle, this is Miss Starling, the new cook. My daughter, Gayle.' Meecham introduced them smoothly. Gayle gave the cook a smile that was pleasant enough, but which was distinctly distracted. She caught her father's eye, and Meecham, reading her look instantly, wordlessly excused himself and moved away.

Father and daughter retired to one corner.

'They'll all be here in a minute,' Elsie muttered behind her, her broad country accent very agreeable on the ear.

'All?'

'Everyone comes down here,' Elsie said, 'save for their nibs. It's warm you see. And cosy. And the old cook always had scones or cake or summat about that you could nibble on.'

Elsie gauged the new cook to be in her late twenties, or at a push, early thirties. She looked far too young, anyway, to be able to cope. But Jenny instantly and gratefully took the hint. As soon as she'd planned and begun the evening meal, she'd get onto it. The kitchen was expected, it seemed, to keep a constant source of cakes and buns on hand. So be it.

Over in the corner, Jenny saw Gayle Meecham shake her head vehemently. She didn't look happy, but her father was obviously winning whatever argument they were having. Eventually, Gayle sighed and left, but, as she opened the door to go, a bubble of energy burst through it, dressed in a paint-smeared smock, and with long brown hair flying. Gayle very wisely stood aside to let the human dynamo in.

'Hello, Meech. Anything good to eat? I'm starving!'

Jenny instantly felt stricken. The very words 'I'm starving' struck instantly at her heart, like a skewer. And uttered by a growing girl, they were doubly pathetic.

'I'll have some toasted sandwiches ready in a jiffy,' she promised automatically. They were the only things that were hot, filling, and could be made in next to no time.

'Lady Roberta, this is Miss Starling, the new cook,' Meecham introduced them, unfazed by being referred to as 'Meech'.

'Hello there,' the brown-haired, paint-smeared energy bundle said, and quickly plopped down into one of the padded chairs. Behind her came a young man, rather less paint smeared, who made straight for the fire. He was tall, lean, and looked slightly effete. One could imagine him in an amateur dramatics society playing Byron, or one of those tragic, doomed young men. He was so handsome he almost hurt the eyes.

Roberta, Jenny noticed, even over the bread and cheese she was preparing, never took her eyes off him, and she hid the small smile tugging at her lips by turning to the grill.

'Would you like a toasted sandwich, Mr Powell-Brooks?' Jenny asked, and the young art tutor turned, no doubt surprised to be addressed by a stranger.

'Oh, no, thank you. Unlike some greedy little monkey I can mention, I can actually hold out until dinner.'

Roberta grinned then pouted. 'Killjoy,' she said, then added, 'Oh, Malc, I've used up all the red. You remember that sunset I did last night?'

Malcolm Powell-Brooks looked over at his young pupil, a smile of resigned exasperation on his face. 'What, *all* the red? What did you apply it with? A shovel?'

'What's that about a shovel?' a new voice asked, and Jenny turned to see the pretty blonde maid come in. Tomorrow she would have to start baking some good solid cakes—caraway seed cake. Walnut and coffee perhaps. Even if she had only this minute arrived, she felt as if she were failing them all by being unable to produce scones from out of thin air.

'Lady Roberta, your Henry has been up to his usual shenanigans again,' the maid reproached mildly. It was obvious that the servants at the castle enjoyed a friendly and relaxed atmosphere with their employers, no doubt due to long association.

Janice really was extraordinarily pretty, Jenny thought, as she removed the toasted cheese from the grill, cut it into triangles, added some Worcestershire sauce and sliced tomato on top and presented it to Lady Roberta, who took it with a face-splitting grin and instantly tucked in.

Jenny guessed that Janice's job was to keep his lordship and Lady Vee's private living area clean and polished, and that a small army of villagers came in to see to the rest of the castle.

Jenny watched, bemused, as her solitary diner consumed the still sizzling cheese with satisfying gusto. Her gums, Jenny thought absently, must come iron-plated.

'Oh Henry. He gets everywhere,' Roberta said airily between mouthfuls. 'I was only five when I had him, Miss Starling,' she explained, taking it for granted that the new cook would know what she was talking about. 'At that age, I thought a tortoise would be amazing fun.

But old Courts, the gardener, he fenced off all the vegetable gardens so that Henry couldn't get in and munch his grotty old lettuces. So Henry gets bored, and in the summer he sticks his big fat nose in everywhere. Can't blame him, I suppose. In winter, he just disappears. Under the stairs, I expect, or one of the airing cupboards. Nobody's ever found out where he goes.'

'Mr Courtenay was quite right to keep that animal out,' Elsie surprised Jenny by piping up. 'And you like his grotty lettuces right enough, your ladyship, when they come in a salad.'

Roberta grinned, totally unabashed. 'Quite right too, Else.'

Jenny, recognizing the young lady's penchant for shortening names, wondered what she'd come up with in her case. Was she doomed to be called Jen, or maybe even Old Star for the rest of Roberta's residency? The thought made her shudder.

Meecham had now wandered back from his conference with his daughter, and accepted a cup of tea. When the kitchen door once again opened and closed with an echoing thud, everyone looked around. But the woman who walked in seemed not to notice that she was momentarily the focus of all eyes, and made her way calmly to the table.

Jenny judged her to be in her early thirties. She had short, but nicely cut, wavy dark-blonde hair and a heart-shaped face. Big blue eyes looked out on the world with a kind of unkind wisdom that made the cook feel instantly uncomfortable. She should have been quite beautiful, but somehow, wasn't.

'I see we have a new arrival,' the newcomer said, her voice flat and even and curiously bland.

'Jenny Starling,' Jenny said, thrusting out her hand and finding it taken in a warm strong grip.

'I'm Ava Simmons, Lady Roberta's governess.'

Jenny, who remembered seeing her on the stairs not an hour ago studying a painting, nodded politely.

'Simm, want a sandwich?' Roberta asked, quickly biting into the last one of hers, lest someone take her seriously.

Ava Simmons smiled at her pupil in genuine fondness. 'No, thank you, Lady Roberta. I'm quite sure I can wait for my dinner.' The gentle reproof, much to the cook's relief, slid right off Roberta's back like water off a duck's feathers. (Jenny liked to see people eat.)

Without asking, Ava helped herself to a cup of tea, and seated herself at the table, sipping gently. No one spoke. Slightly puzzled at the abruptly repressed atmosphere that seemed to have settled over everybody, Jenny felt the sudden need to dent the silence.

'Have you worked here long, Miss Simmons?' she asked, and the governess gave her a grateful look.

'No, just over two weeks. Lady Vee and Sir George decided that, at sixteen, Lady Roberta's school lessons should gradually give way to rather broader experiences.'

'She means,' Roberta said, rolling her eyes, 'that their nibs want me to walk and talk like a lady. Good old Simm has me pacing the nursery with books on my head.'

Everybody smiled as they pictured the absurd spectacle. And yet Jenny had detected just a hint of asperity in Lady Roberta's voice. It also explained the awkward silence. Miss Simmons was new to the job, and it would take her a while to fit into the tight niche that no doubt existed here.

As cook, Jenny's own acceptance was taken a little more for granted. No one wanted to get on the bad side of the cook, after all. They could end up with lumpy gravy and burnt chops.

'That reminds me,' Malcolm Powell-Brooks said, out of the blue. 'That skylight needs to be widened in the studio. We're not getting enough light. Do you think you could get some workmen in, Meecham?'

Meecham nodded, and promised to get onto it. Ava Simmons sighed. 'You should see the studio, Miss Starling. It would put a professional artist to shame.'

'Only the best for my pupil,' Malcolm said, but his jaunty smile seemed just a little bit strained. 'When you're teaching the granddaughter of a family of art collectors like the Avonsleighs, only the finest canvases, best paints and most professional brushes will do. Right, Rob?'

Lady Roberta grinned, hoist by her own petard. She pouted again. 'Rob, indeed,' she muttered, but her eyes sparkled and looked adoringly on the visage of her idol.

Ava Simmons looked away, frowning slightly, and Jenny wanted to tell her not to worry—that sixteen-year-old girls were apt to get crushes on their teachers, especially ones who looked like Malcolm Powell-Brooks. Nothing ever came of it.

Usually.

'Besides, I'm going to be a great artist someday,' Lady Roberta said, with all the confidence of a teenager. 'I'll be the first really famous female artist ever. Have you noticed how all the really famous ones are men, Miss Starling?'

Jenny, grateful to be spared any shortening of her name, smiled. 'I hadn't really thought about it.'

'Well, they are,' Roberta said sulkily. 'It's all right for Malc. He could make a name for himself if he wanted, just because he's a man. But nobody takes a woman artist seriously.'

'Now you know that's not true,' Malcolm said with a gentle smile. 'We've studied some of the women artists. Besides, you know that I don't paint professionally. Just because I got a degree from the Ruskin, doesn't mean I have talent. You can be taught to appreciate fine art, but that doesn't make you an artist. Right, Ava?' he suddenly turned and smiled full-face at the governess.

To Jenny's surprise, Ava Simmons went extremely pale. At the same time, she distinctly heard Elsie give a snicker, over by the kettle, where she was making some fresh tea. Ava managed a strained smile. 'Quite. My father owns the Giselle Gallery in Bicester,' Ava said, for the new cook's benefit. 'As a teenager, I, too, wanted to go to the Ruskin School of Fine Art at Oxford, but it didn't work out.'

'Poor Simm,' Roberta said, looking genuinely sorry for her.

'You see what I mean? Nobody takes women artists seriously. But I'm going to be famous one day, with Malc's help. I am good, aren't I, Malc?' she asked, turning such pleading eyes up to her tutor that Jenny again felt her own lips twitch.

Malcolm Powell-Brooks walked over and gave her head an affection pat. 'Not bad, little monkey. You're not bad at all.'

Roberta, obviously not best pleased at being treated so openly like a child sighed heavily. Ava Simmons scowled and looked away. Everyone tactfully turned their attention back to their tea. The air seemed to grow heavy and oppressed.

And Jenny, with a trickle of unease, wondered if things were always this tense at Avonsleigh Castle.

She hoped not. Souffles never rose in a tense kitchen.

THREE

JENNY WALKED ACROSS to the oven, donning thick oven gloves as she went. Keenly aware of her audience, she withdrew a massive Lancashire hotpot from the middle tray. This was the staff's dish of course, designed to feed seven. Steaming and heavy, she transferred it onto a wooden stand on the sideboard, where Elsie was waiting, nose twitching, ready to dish it out.

Being interviewed in the morning, accepting the job, and then cooking her first meal all on the same day had been a challenge, and one she'd thought about carefully. And, mindful of her promise to her employers, she had decided to cook something very English, delicious and filling.

The rich aroma soon filled the kitchen, and behind her she could almost feel the others relax. Once more at the oven, she removed the second smaller hotpot, and Meecham instantly commandeered it. Heaping a variety of green vegetables into a dish, she watched as Meecham added it to an enormous silver tray.

She'd already ascertained from Elsie that Lady Vee and Lord Avonsleigh weren't overly keen on too many courses (except when entertaining) but still wondered if she ought to have at least made some soup, or another kind of starter. But it was too late to worry about that now.

At the table, with the hotpot and vegetables now ladled out, there was a very satisfactory silence. Jenny
took her seat at the head of the table, as befitting her
position, and took her first bite. It was, as she'd always
known it would be, delicious.

'Is Danny coming over tonight, Janice?' Gayle Meecham asked, reaching for a glass of water and taking
a sip. Janice swallowed a good mouthful of food, and
nodded.

'About eight, he said. Not that we're going anywhere
special. Just down to the Jolly Farmer. Still, it gets me
out of this place,' she said cheerfully and tucked in
once more, and with evident enjoyment. Jenny rather
approved of Janice.

Opposite her, Ava Simmons raised her napkin and
gave her lips a gentle pat before reaching for a small
glass of wine. Up a place, and opposite, Elsie watched
the governess with derisive eyes. Malcolm Powell-
Brooks waited patiently for his food to cool. Lady Roberta, of course, ate with her grandparents. No doubt
she'd much rather eat down here with the servants who
were her friends, Jenny suspected, and, of course, with
her art tutor, who must be the cause of many a blush-
making, teenage dream.

'I'd have thought you'd want to meet him at the pub
rather than have him come up here, Janice,' Malcolm
said, and smiled mischievously as her pretty blonde
head shot up. Both of them turned and glanced at Ava
Simmons, who seemed oblivious to it all.

Jenny noticed Janice flush a dull, unbecoming red,
but before she could make any gentle probing as to
what Malcolm was insinuating, Meecham reappeared.

In spite of herself, Jenny was uncomfortably aware that she was watching him anxiously. Noticing her scrutiny, he smiled gently.

'Their lordships would like to express their approval and satisfaction, Miss Starling,' the butler said in his usual pedantic tone. Translated—they had lifted the lid, taken one delighted look, and tucked in like gannets.

Jenny beamed, and for the first time that evening, fully relaxed. She glanced over her shoulder to the stove and the two big pots, steaming away gently, and glanced at the kitchen clock. Perfect timing. The two raspberry jam steamed puddings would be cooked to perfection in another fifteen minutes.

'Has anyone seen my knitting needle? My number ten?' Elsie suddenly piped up, her voice abrupt and accusing. 'I know I had it the day before yesterday. I was knitting a cardigan for Bunty's youngest.'

'Are you sure it's not in your bag, Elsie?' Gayle asked, ignoring the exasperated looks the others cast in the kitchen maid's direction.

Elsie's unlovely face became set. 'No, it ain't. First place I looked, weren't it? It's not there. The other one is. Someone must have took it, that's all.'

'Who'd want to steal just one knitting needle, Elsie?' Janice piped up reasonably. 'Perhaps it went the same way as that slipper of yours.' She glanced across at Jenny, and winked. 'Or that thimble you swore somebody had pinched.'

Elsie merely glowered. 'Someone put that slipper under my chair. I never does that. I always has me slippers on, else they're kept under me bed. I know who it was, all right. That young ladyship. Little minx. Thinks I don't know where I put things. But I ain't so daft. And that thimble shouldn't have been in that drawer. I never keeps me thimbles in that drawer.'

'Oh well, I'm sure it will turn up, Elsie,' Gayle said placatingly.

When everybody had finished, Jenny did a quick check of the plates. Elsie, Meecham, Janice and Gayle had left clean plates. Only Malcolm and Ava Simmons had left some, mostly vegetables. All in all, she was satisfied.

'That's the bell, Dad,' Gayle said, prompting her father as a faint but plainly audible bell tinkled overhead. So Meecham was just a little hard of hearing, Jenny noted idly. Or was he just preoccupied?

The butler followed her to the stove and watched with evident approval as she removed the family's pudding from the pot, took off the greaseproof paper, traced a knife around the edge and upturned it. The sponge came out clean, golden and light, the generous helping of runny, piping hot jam trickling down the sides in a delicious stream. A jug of proper custard was placed by its side and Meecham left, moving at a fair old clip. When she turned back to the stove, Jenny was just in time to see Elsie already turning out the larger servants' bowl onto a plate.

The cook hadn't heard her, and for a moment, she felt slightly uneasy. She *should* have heard her crossing the flagged kitchen floor. She *should* have heard her lifting the lid and clattering about. As she watched the tired-looking maid at work, she realized that Elsie was deceptively deft. Her movements were slow but graceful. Now wonder she moved and worked so silently.

Jenny would have to remember that.

Once again, the table was silent as everybody tucked in, according to his or her manner. The staff were now beginning to solidify into distinct personalities: Elsie, with her habit of losing knick-knacks and complaining; Janice, with her healthy appetite and content, slightly smug, beauty; Ava, a lady born and bred, and perhaps a little resentful that she had to earn her living; Malcolm, the fastidious, slightly spiteful art tutor; and Meecham, a kind-hearted man, who seemed to fit in at Avonsleigh like a key fitting into a lock. Only Gayle seemed to remain a mystery. Protective of Elsie, yes; kind-hearted, like her father no doubt. But Jenny, as yet, knew next to nothing about her. What went on behind that aloof exterior? And was it her imagination, or was Gayle upset about something?

Meecham returned, gave the cook another smiling nod, and had just sat down when the door burst open and a young man athletically leapt down the steps, landing nearly in the middle of the kitchen. He was dressed in a heavy leather jacket and carried a crash helmet in his hand. *See me, I have a motor bike. Aren't I wild*? His hair was windblown, jet black and flopped about on his forehead, forcing him to keep brushing it back. The newcomer's jaw was busy chewing gum. 'Hello, Jan. Troops.' He nodded to the rest of the table, his glance stopping at Ava Simmons. 'Ava, you're looking ravishing tonight,' he said, his blue eyes twinkling down at her.

'Daniel,' Ava Simmons said, barely turning her head.

'Danny, want some of my pudding?' Janice put in quickly, and hitched up a spare chair beside her. Danny obliged, but turned the chair around, sitting on it so that the back of it rested against his chest. He looked too old to be playing those sort of games, Jenny thought with a hint of asperity, looking at him closely. He was no teenager. More in the mid-twenties, she would guess. He accepted Janice's pudding, totally unaware of the sacrifice she was making, and spooned in a gigantic mouthful. It made even Jenny blink.

Elsie was watching him closely too, Jenny noticed, and felt a slight shudder of shock. Surely Elsie, of all people, wasn't attracted by this show of swaggering machismo? But no, she saw an instant later, Elsie wasn't. She was watching him with a kind of superior smile that changed to the now familiar smirk, when the conceited Danny once more glanced Ava Simmons' way.

Janice, not liking the way his eyes tended to stray either, pulled on his arm. 'I'm ready for the off, Danny. Where's the bike?'

'Near the gatehouse, of course, where else? I can't drive it into the quad, can I?' Janice flushed. 'Hey, Ava, want to take a ride on my Harley? It's got a really wide seat,' he cajoled.

Jenny heard a distinct giggle. Or titter. It could have come from almost anyone, for she was not alone in realizing what an incongruous picture Danny's offer conjured up—the genteel and proper Miss Simmons on the back of a motorbike.

Ava smiled, not too unkindly, Jenny thought, given

the circumstances. 'Thank you, Daniel. But I don't have a helmet.'

Very tactful, Jenny thought idly.

Danny seemed not to recognize the dismissal however, and shook off Janice's hand, which had tightened annoyingly around his wrist. 'I can get you one. I'll bring one over next week.'

'Danny,' Janice said, drawing out his name into two very long, very annoyed syllables.

'All right, all right, I'm coming. Just let me finish this pud. Good stuff, this,' he added, finishing off the desert in three giant, jaw-breaking mouthfuls.

They all watched the unlikely lovebirds depart, Meecham and his daughter with some amusement, Malcolm more with exasperation than anything else. Elsie merely sneered. It was, Jenny was coming to realize, the kitchen maid's near-permanent expression.

A HALF-HOUR LATER, she and Elsie set about clearing and washing up, managing to finish the work in a matter of minutes. They divided their tasks equally and automatically, working in a comfortable silence. She had just wiped down the largest bowl, and was about to put it back in the cupboard, when Meecham coughed discreetly behind her. She looked back over her shoulder, and raised an eyebrow.

'Lady Vee and Sir George would like to see you, Miss Starling. In the sunroom.'

Jenny nodded, put down the bowl on the shelf, and heard a curious, not to mention ominous, dull thunk.

Curious, she peered into the recess of the cupboard, saw something move, and reached inside.

When her hands emerged, she was holding Henry.

For a second the reptile blinked at her, and she blinked back at it. Then, without a word, she carefully put it on the floor, returned the bowl to its proper place, and turned to follow Meecham. She spared only a moment to wonder how the tortoise had got onto the cupboard shelf, which was a least three feet off the ground.

But her thoughts were mainly centred on the upcoming meeting. Perhaps the family hadn't been as happy with the food as Meecham had led her to believe? Had Elsie lied when she said they didn't go in for lots of courses when they dined alone? So nervous was she, she barely glanced at her surroundings as Meecham led her down the maze-like corridors to a small room decorated in pale yellow. The butler bowed silently, and left.

Her ladyship looked up from a surprisingly garish tabloid newspaper and beamed. 'Ah, Miss Starling, there you are. I just wanted to say what a delightful meal that was. Haven't had Lancashire hotpot for ages. Our old cook was from Devon, you know.'

Jenny didn't, but didn't care. She hadn't been told politely to sling her hook, and that was all that mattered.

'Lovely puddin',' his lordship rumbled in agreement from the depths of an old armchair, without bothering to open his firmly shut eyes.

'George always naps after dinner,' said Lady Vee, anxious that the new cook should not take offence. Not after the meal they'd just had. 'I just wanted to say how much we enjoyed it, and also to warn you that we're expecting friends tomorrow for tea.'

'Not dinner?' Jenny asked quickly.

'No, just tea. Well, not even that really. The colonel and his wife will be arriving about three, I expect, so if you could just have a little something ready. Just a scone or two, would be fine. The colonel's got a bit of a thing about dining out. Can't stand to do it. His poor wife hasn't eaten in a restaurant for twenty years.'

Jenny nodded. And she knew better than to be fooled by this 'just a scone or two' business. 'Some Madeira cake, perhaps?' she murmured. 'And the odd savoury? Some small egg and bacon flans—cold, of course—and some sandwiches? Cucumber, egg and cress? I'll bake some fresh bread after lunch.'

Her ladyship beamed. 'Splendid, splendid. Well, I won't keep you. You must be exhausted. I can't tell you how grateful we are, can I, George, that you were able to start work straight away.' In answer, a loud snore came from the depths of his lordship's chair.

Jenny smiled, and withdrew. Once the door was shut behind her she found herself in a small anteroom. Wryly, she realized that she had been too worried to take notice of all the twists and turns in getting here and was now thoroughly lost. She glanced around her at the now expected plethora of paintings, and lingered over a charming picture of water lilies on a misty lake. But as she slowly walked off in what she hoped was the right direction, a gleam of jewellike light caught her eye, and she turned back, glancing up in surprise. For there on the wall above her, was the most beautiful—and outlandish—work of art she'd ever seen. A lavishly jewelled dagger, with a narrow, straight blade, hung in solitary splendour in a little alcove in one wall.

As she looked at it, so beautiful and so deadly, she felt a shiver run over her spine. It was an unexpectedly strong shiver, and it raised goose bumps on her arm. A feeling of foreboding crept into the back of her mind, and she briskly, almost angrily, pushed it back.

Nothing was going to go wrong, she told herself. Not this time. Besides, she had other things to think about.

Like tea for four tomorrow. And a finicky colonel with a phobia about food. Perhaps she should make some little crab patties. Maybe a few lemon slices....

FOUR

JENNY AWOKE, surrounded by four posts, swathes of electric blue silk, and a feeling of well-being. The bed beneath her was wide and well padded, and supported her Junoesque figure admirably, and for a moment she lay in blissful silence. Already, Avonsleigh felt like home. She and Lady Vee had an understanding that was as strong as only two like-minded women could make it. She had an able, if sour, helper in Elsie, and the butler was a man of understanding. A perfect recipe for longstanding and satisfying employment, if ever she'd heard it.

And now for breakfast. She glanced at her watch, found it was only 6.30, and smiled. Traditional English breakfast of course—bacon, sausages, tomatoes (if the greenhouses had any), eggs fresh from the hen house and those kidneys she'd discovered yesterday at the back of the fridge. Now who, she mused, had tried to hide *them* away?

Lunch at the castle was always a simple affair—something light or just sandwiches, Elsie had told her. And the trick to good sandwiches, Jenny knew, was variety and properly baked bread. But today there was this tea, that wasn't really tea, but a chance for her new employers to show off their new cook to their—hopefully—suitably envious friends.

Jenny stretched in bliss, contemplating a full day's cooking ahead of her, yawned extravagantly, then rolled out of bed. She quickly washed, dressed, and brushed her cap of dark, shining hair into tidy order. In the bedroom's large and anciently spotted mirror, her blue eyes shone.

Little onion tarts. She'd have a quick tour of the river that meandered through the outlying meadows and see if she could find some watercress. Make some mayonnaise. Yes, she had a busy day ahead. Just how she liked it. And then there was dinner.

Jenny was still contemplating dinner when she reached the kitchen and found Elsie already ensconced and inevitably drinking tea. 'Good morning, Elsie. You're an early riser, I see.'

Elsie grunted, but was already on her feet and pouring out another cup. 'Usual breakfast then?' she asked, as she watched Jenny set about the frying pans and checking the vegetable oil.

'Yes. The sausage skins need puncturing, please, and be sure to give the bacon rind a good scoring. Does the family like their bacon crispy?'

'Ahh. His lordship likes his practically burned.'

'OK.' Jenny relaxed over her first cup of tea, and thought about dinner. Steak and onion pie, mashed potatoes, boiled with sprigs of mint, glazed carrots and diced swede, lightly buttered. And for his lordship's pudding? Well, she'd promised him rhubarb and custard, so that settled it.

Outside, the sun began to shine as if it meant it for the first time in a week, so she set about opening all the windows and side doors leading out to the vegetable gardens. Her menu was planned, the sun was shining, and Elsie was firmly in her corner. Nothing could go wrong now.

She should have known better. She really should.

'AHH, MISS STARLING,' her ladyship said, her usual greeting now causing not a hint of panic in the cook. 'That breakfast was superb.'

'Good bacon,' Lord Avonsleigh grunted, over his paper and toast. She had been called to the breakfast-room just before nine o'clock. She was glad she hadn't put the bread in the oven yet. She liked to keep an eye on that.

'About Colonel and Mrs Attling. I thought, since the weather's changed, we'd have it out on the terrace,' Lady Vee swept on. 'Normally, when we entertain friends we do it in the sunroom, it has such a pleasant aspect, but the colonel spent a lot of time in the Far East, you know, and simply can't stand to be indoors if the sun is shining.'

Jenny nodded sympathetically in understanding. 'Lemonade?' she hazarded softly, and Lady Vee beamed.

'Mrs Attling is so fond of it,' she agreed. 'I'll tell Meecham about the change of venue. If you could have everything ready for three?'

Jenny nodded. 'Three it is,' she murmured.

Back in the kitchen, with the staff's breakfast cleared away, the day began for her in earnest. It also began in earnest for others.

A killer among them....

Upstairs, in a large and airy room that Lady Roberta rather liked, she watched Miss Simmons pace about in front of her. On the CD player was a Bach concerto that neither of them was listening to, although Roberta knew she'd be asked questions about it afterwards.

Roberta glanced at her watch. Another hour and a half and she would be with Malcolm. What would he make of her sunset painting? Would he lean over behind her, right up close, to point something out, as he sometimes did? Roberta hoped so. She could smell his aftershave if he did that, and his cheek was so close to hers that she could touch it, if she suddenly swung her head around. Although he was getting wise to that trick, she remembered mournfully. Still, sometimes his shoulder would touch hers, and the shivers that went through her were delicious.

'Listen carefully to this piano piece, Lady Roberta. I have the music sheet for it somewhere, and we'll see how well you can play it this afternoon.' Roberta nodded attentively. Then glanced at her watch. An hour and a quarter. Ava Simmons continued her pacing, her brow deeply furrowed.

Lady Roberta's tutor was in fact, deep in thought. Tomorrow he would come, and then…. Well, then she would act. She didn't want to do it. The whole thing was so distasteful. But she had never shirked her responsibilities, and she wouldn't start now. Other women might jib at doing what she was going to do, but she was made of sterner stuff. She had faced a lot of unpleasantness in her short life. With her father being like he was—a monster—and her mother abandoning her when she was but twelve—yes, Ava Simmons was made of strong stuff indeed.

IN HER LADYSHIP's bedroom, Gayle Meecham reached for the afternoon dress that Lady Vee had selected, and took it to the dressing-room. There she put on the iron, and waited for it to heat up. When the family chose to entertain family and friends, Gayle would usually act as an extra maid.

The butler's daughter sighed deeply and ran a hand across her forehead. She had a headache, but that was not unusual. Just lately, her head seemed to be perpetually throbbing. If only she'd had the courage to disobey her father yesterday morning. Nothing good would come of what they were planning. She knew it, deep inside. It was nasty, there was no other word for it. As she'd tried to tell him yesterday, two wrongs did not make a right. They never had, they never would. But would he listen? Which meant that now she had no choice. Her father was a clever man in many ways. He managed the running of the castle—and his lordship—with tact and gentle aplomb. But when it came to the realities of the world…. Well, her father needed Avonsleigh as much as Avonsleigh needed him. He couldn't really exist in the outside world. Which was why, when the outside world had come crashing into their lives just weeks ago, she knew it would be up to her to look after him.

He would never get away with what he was planning without her help. He simply had no real flair for villainy. At heart, he was a gentle man. But a man obsessed. It was such a dangerous combination. And she wished, oh she *wished*, that he would change his mind.

It would happen today, or more likely tomorrow. And once that initial step had been taken, there would be no going back.

She reached for the iron and absent-mindedly tested it with her finger. An instant later, she gave a small cry and pulled her hand away quickly. The iron was red-hot. Too hot for the dress, and she quickly turned the dial down a few notches.

It was not like her to be so careless.

For a long while, Gayle Meecham stared at her burnt finger, her headache gradually getting worse.

UP IN THE studio, Malcolm Powell-Brooks stared at the painting in front of him. He'd been working on it all morning, safe in the knowledge that Roberta was being kept firmly out of the way by the redoubtable Ava. His lips twisted as he stared at the grey and green land-scape on his easel. It was not good enough. He knew it. Hell, any second-rate first year art student would know it was no good.

With an angry sigh he threw down his paintbrush and walked to the window. Damn it all. He was just so distracted and unable to concentrate. He was worried. And scared. Oh yes, he thought grimly, he was scared. Damn her!

JANICE GAVE THE huge Ming vase a final flick with her duster and turned away, uncharacteristically oblivious of the fact that her duster had just caused to wobble a vase worth nearly £10,000.

The ubiquitous treasures of Avonsleigh might make the occasional museum executive gasp in delight, but Janice was mostly oblivious to the art around her. She came from a big family, and had moved out of her parents' cramped council house just as quickly as she'd been able to, so she was grateful for her large room at the castle, and the peace and quiet she enjoyed in her hours off.

Today, though, she was in no mood to count her blessings. She knew what Danny was up to. Oh yes, she knew. She was nowhere near as stupid as some people liked to think. And she wouldn't let him get away with it. She was meeting him this afternoon, and she would have it out with him once and for all. If he thought she was going to stand for it, he'd better think again. Nobody messed Janice Beale about.

She was pretty enough to have any man she wanted, and it was high time that Danny learned that. She would put a spoke in his wheel, all right. Oh yes, she thought grimly, as she gave an eighteenth-century wall plaque a vigorous dusting. She'd fix his plans, good and proper.

JENNY'S HUGE MOUND of sandwiches dwindled to an empty plate as lunchtime came and went and the staff of Avonsleigh did likewise. Roberta, Jenny noticed, skipped having lunch with her grandparents and tucked in to the watercress and egg mayonnaise sandwiches as if she was ravenous. Meecham, the cook noticed with a slight frown, ate practically nothing. Malcolm was the first to leave the kitchen, but Janice took his place, tucking into egg and watercress and saying very little. Jenny, used to judging people from the perspective of food, began to feel uneasy.

Something was up. It was nothing she could put her finger on, precisely, but there was an undercurrent present today that had been absent yesterday. Or had it been there all the time, and she was only now picking up on it?

'What kind of garden furniture has been set up on the terrace, Mr Meecham?' she asked, determined to break the rather oppressive silence.

Meecham jumped, as if dragged from a vast depth of thought. 'Hmm? Oh, a huge, white-painted, wrought-iron table, solid as a rock. Plenty of room for all your goodies.'

Ava Simmons glanced at the cook and smiled. 'Are you settling in all right, Miss Starling?' she asked thoughtfully, and Jenny smiled.

'Yes, thank you, Miss Simmons. Would you like another sandwich?'

Ava declined with a murmured thanks, and then glanced over at Roberta. 'Lady Roberta, we have those Byron poems to discuss.'

Lady Roberta sighed theatrically, but in truth, didn't mind. She'd found his scandalous life-story rather titillating. Besides, she'd once seen a painting of the poet, and he'd looked a lot like Malcolm. Those same brooding eyes. That same, rakish air of smouldering passion. 'Mad, bad, and dangerous to know,' Roberta quoted Lady Caroline Lamb with a cheeky grin. 'I'm surprised you dare to read him, Simm. Aren't you afraid he'll corrupt me?' she added, her voice just a touch sharp.

Jenny turned in time to see a rather spiteful or, perhaps, *angry* look flit across her young face. Since girls today probably knew more about sex than many of their elders, she wondered why a no doubt very worldly-wise teenager wanted to bait her tutor with something so innocuous.

Ava Simmons, though, merely smiled. 'Glad to see you're using your initiative, Lady Roberta,' she responded smoothly, not a whit put out. 'Not to mention your grandfather's rather excellent library.'

Roberta looked for a moment as if she might stamp her foot in a fit of old-fashioned temper, but then a reluctant smile crossed her face. She really was a likeable teenager, Jenny thought. She might not quite like her tutor, but she certainly respected her. Not many sixteen year olds had that kind of maturity.

As her kitchen emptied once more, the cook turned her thoughts to the important things in life. Onion tarts. Fresh bread. Her feeling of unease was firmly brushed away.

But it would come back. And with a vengeance.

IN THE COOL of the butler's pantry, Meecham reached for an old jam jar that contained his mother's secret recipe. She claimed it could clean the dirt from the devil, and he was inclined to believe her. Many people had remarked on the sparkling quality of the Avonsleigh silver.

Fastidiously rolling up his shirt sleeves, Meecham reached for a clean cloth, dipped it in the pale yellow goo from the jam-jar, and reached for the dagger. For

a moment he admired it, turning it this way and that.
No wonder the colonel always examined it whenever
he came. No doubt it reminded him of long ago days in
Malaysia. Or wherever.

Meecham smeared the handle and began to rub vigorously, using his fingernails to delve into the crev-
ices created by the gems, humming away softly as he
worked. Time flew by, and he jumped when the pantry door flew open and the new cook stood there, looking worried.

'Mr Meecham, we're out of flour! I can't believe it.
Didn't the old cook keep the larder well stocked?'

Miss Starling, Meecham mused, would *never* panic.
Her voice was calm, if just a little high. Jenny was, however, as *close* to panic as she ever came.

The butler smiled. 'The flour is kept in the cellar,
Miss Starling, along with the wine, the root vegetables,
and some of the over-wintering fruit. Elsie will know
where to find it.'

Jenny let out a long, infinitely relieved breath, and
smiled. Of course Elsie would know. She should have
asked her in the first place. She glanced down at the
dagger in his hand, but her mind was on flour. Not on
sudden death.

'Thank you Mr. Meecham,' she said with a quiet,
self-derogatory smile, and withdrew. Crisis over.

Meecham carried on cleaning the dagger. He cleaned
it for a solid hour. Lovingly, and with infinite patience.

AVA SIMMONS GLANCED at her watch, and saw it was two-
thirty. Where was that child? Late as always. Byron
over, she was supposed to meet her here in the music

room after a short break. No doubt she was in the artist's studio, mooning over that man again.

Ava ran a hand along the grand piano, smiling at the perfectly tuned chords that echoed across the room. Both Lady Vee and her husband were tone deaf, but who cared, when they could afford such a piano, and such a room? The tiled floor and plain walls echoed back the sounds of musical instruments perfectly.

Ava sighed enviously and walked with angry patience to the door. She would just have to drag the girl away from Malcolm Powell-Brooks. As usual.

As she opened the door and crossed the short, flagged inner hall, she noticed that the door to the conservatory was open, and she paused, surprised. Old Seth, the head gardener, was always on about the importance of the conservatory being kept at a constant temperature. There were some valuable and quite beautiful orchids in there, she knew, and anybody visiting it always shut the door after them, from the family right down to Elsie. It had become second nature to everybody living at the castle.

With an exasperated sigh, she reached for the door and was about to close it, when she saw someone move inside.

Someone beckoning to her. Curious, Ava Simmons walked in.

COLONEL ATTLING TURNED off his purring Bentley and walked briskly around to his passenger door, opening it for his wife with a distracted air. He was looking forward to talking to old George again. He knew how to fish, too. Perhaps he could wangle a day out on the Avonsleigh trout lake.

His wife looked at his distant expression and smiled indulgently. She smiled again as Meecham met them at the door and led them solemnly through the castle towards the sunroom. In a small hall, both of their hosts were waiting. Mrs Attling ran sharp eyes over Vee's impeccable peach dress and was relieved that she herself had worn mint-green. It could be so embarrassing, even amongst old friends, to clash with one's hostess. Colour-wise, that was. 'Vee, dear.'

'Millie! So glad you could come. We have a new cook at last!' her ladyship began, cutting to the crux of the matter immediately. Millicent, too, was a gastronome of similar taste, and both women had been worrying about the lack of a cook at Avonsleigh.

'You look pleased with her,' Millicent said, ignoring her husband who had stopped in his usual place, to admire the usual item.

'I am. She's a treasure. Just you wait….' The two women moved off, chattering like well-bred magpies, so that his lordship and the colonel could begin their own pleasures.

'I still wish you'd sell it, old chap,' the colonel said, staring up at the jewelled dagger with envious, covetous eyes. 'I know the old pension doesn't stretch too far these days, but I have the odd acre or two on the estate I could sell off.'

Lord Avonsleigh laughed. 'You could no more sell your land than I could dismiss Meecham, Bill, you old fraud,' he chortled, and the colonel laughed in agreement. Nevertheless, he gave the dagger a last, yearning glance before following his old friend through to the sunroom to join the ladies on the terrace beyond.

Behind him, a huge grandfather clock boomed out the hour of three o'clock.

'Damn thing's deafening,' his lordship muttered over the roar, and the colonel laughed.

'What good's a clock for, if you can't hear it, eh?' he bellowed back.

On the terrace, the sun shone with such pleasant strength that Lady Vee quickly raised the parasol positioned in the centre of the table. The two men elected to sit fully in the sun.

'I do love this little garden,' Millicent said, looking around. Lavateria bushes thrust pink blooms into all corners of the small square, whilst a lavish rose bed was surrounded by a diamond of perfectly clipped boxed yew. Directly facing them was the conservatory, and Millicent let her eyes wander over it. 'Is that a new orchid I can see growing there, Agnes dear?' she asked, pointing to the glass house and a spray of creamy blooms.

Lady Vee smiled. 'It's Seth's passion. Orchids and something else unpronounceable. I like to indulge him. He grows such wonderful onions.'

Meecham coughed, as if on cue, and placed on the table a huge selection of goodies. Onion flans, large sandwiches (with the crusts still on, of course) overflowing with tender ham, home-made chutney and lettuce. Sausage rolls, warm and flaky from the oven. A large Madeira cake eclipsed a slightly smaller fruitcake.

A huge glass jug full of real lemonade, filled with ice and trickling with condensation set everyone's parched throat contracting in happy anticipation.

The colonel's wife and Lady Vee looked at one another without saying a word.

No words were needed.

A real cook, at last!

Then they smiled as the colonel, eyeing the delicious fare, said haltingly, 'I say, that looks rather good. Perhaps I might just try one of those eggy flan things.'

Half an hour later only some Madeira cake remained on the table, and Meecham, retrieving the depleted tray, smiled happily. Miss Starling would be pleased.

'How about a game of billiards, Bill?' Avonsleigh asked, knowing his friend well, and the two men rose with some alacrity.

Lady Vee also rose. 'It's getting rather warm out here, Millie. Why don't we…?' she murmured happily. As a group, and led by the impassive Meecham, they all trooped through the sunroom and back into the hall.

There it was Meecham who stopped first, and so abruptly that the colonel almost rear-ended him. 'I say, Meecham old chap,' he began, then stopped as he took a proper look at the man. The butler stood stock still, staring up and to his left, his jaw literally dropping open. As a spectacle, it was unparalleled.

The colonel quickly followed the other man's gaze, and blinked. His own jaw quickly followed Meecham's example.

For on the wall, the jewelled dagger gleamed in the sunlight. But nobody, for once, was looking at its spectacular gems. Because, dripping from its blade and running in a small, ragged trail down the white wall, was a thin trickle of thick, red liquid.

Lady Vee and Lord Avonsleigh gaped.

Mrs Attling also stared, and was the first to speak. 'Why, it looks like blood,' she said, the final word almost a whisper.

The grandfather clock boomed the half-hour and broke the spell that had held them all in a frozen tableau of stiff-limbed, wide-eyed disbelief.

It also made everyone jump out of their collective skins.

'Meecham, you'd better....' his lordship paused, thought, and then said, more strongly. 'Meecham, check the household. See if anyone is missing.'

Meecham, with some effort, pulled his glance away from the dagger, blinked once, and then pulled himself together. 'Yes m'lord,' he said quietly. 'At once.'

'Let's go back into the sunroom,' Lady Vee suggested, her booming voice for once subdued. 'I suddenly feel rather chilly.'

The colonel went quickly to his wife and guided her inside, and the two men exchanged worried glances over the top of her head. It *had* looked uncommonly like blood. Ridiculous of course. At Avonsleigh, of all places. And yet....

A few minutes later, Meecham returned. He looked deadly pale. His eyes were round and enormous. He cleared his throat, but his lordship was already on his feet.

'I'm afraid sir, that the tutor, Miss Simmons, is in the conservatory,' Meecham said.

His words were so innocuous that for a moment George wanted to laugh. Then, seeing his butler sway slightly, he snapped sharply, 'So what, man? She can be in the conservatory if she wants to be.'

'Yes, m'lord, I know,' Meecham said. 'But she's dead.'

FIVE

DETECTIVE INSPECTOR JOHN Bishop looked up as the castle loomed into view, and felt his mouth go slightly dry. By his side, Sergeant Myers concentrated on his driving. Behind them was a police van packed with forensic people and SOCOs.

'Shall I pull into the castle proper, sir?' Myers asked, and the inspector nodded.

'Might as well.'

A moment later, they pulled up beside a rather handsome Bentley and stepped out. Immediately a pair of massive double doors swung open with what looked like surprising ease, and a butler stood there. He looked, the inspector thought, rather pale and wide-eyed, but apart from that, he was the picture of an impeccable English manservant—surely a dying breed nowadays. He even coughed discreetly, just in case he had gone unnoticed.

Bishop and Myers approached, the scene-of-crime men not far behind. 'Good afternoon, sir,' Meecham addressed the taller, stockier man instinctively.

'And you are?' Bishop asked, not sharply, not softly.

'Meecham, sir, the family's butler. His lordship asked if he might see you right away. He and her ladyship are in the Turner lounge.'

Bishop felt his neck muscles stiffen. And so it begins,

he thought miserably. The aristocracy, asserting their power. Making sure that he knew he was only a humble copper, whilst they were the Avonsleighs, who were to be obeyed and waited upon, even by British officialdom.

He knew he'd have to cope with this inferiority complex problem of his, ever since the extraordinary call had come in to his office in Kidlington, where the Thames Valley Police had their headquarters. Not that they got calls like that every day. A killing at Avonsleigh Castle! He had barely put down the phone when his superior had called, demanding that he act with tact, discretion and the proper respect. All very well, Bishop thought. But just how *did* you treat a peer of the realm when someone had just bumped off their granddaughter's governess in their conservatory? He felt as if he'd wandered into a game of Cluedo!

Whatever comes or goes, Bishop thought grimly, they had to be included on the list of suspects at least, if not openly questioned as such. Damned if he knew how to go about it though. Still, he was a policeman, and the sooner he stamped his authority onto the scene, the better. 'My sergeant and I will be glad to come, sir, but I want these gentlemen shown to the scene of the crime at once.'

Meecham merely nodded, and glanced behind him. 'Gayle, can you take the gentlemen to the conservatory?' As he spoke, a younger female version of himself stepped out of the shadows and appeared in the doorway behind him.

'Certainly. Would you come this way please?' Her voice was as cool and controlled as she herself looked.

Bishop, his sergeant and the butler stepped out of the way to allow the forensic boys through, and watched as the white-suited team followed the girl into the cavernous interior of the great hall. They made an odd, solemn procession and, for a moment, Bishop felt as if he'd just stepped back a few centuries.

It was an eerie feeling.

'This way, sir,' Meecham said, stepping back into the vast, flagstoned hall with its dominant chandelier, guarded by the empty suits of armour.

Bishop tried his best to be unaffected by all the history, but failed rather miserably. The castle, he knew had stood for centuries, and the influence of the Avonsleighs was felt for miles around, in every circle of rural life. His lordship owned the village of Upper Caulcott, lock, stock and barrel. Farms for miles around occupied his land, and were worked by his tenants. He was a JP, and sat on practically every local influential committee there was going. His wife lead the WI, was active in church circles, and was widely respected by all the local women. Their power was solid and ethereal—hard to define, but impossible to deny.

By his side, Myers adjusted his tie, proof that not even he was immune to the atmosphere of might the castle seemed to ooze from its very walls. Here I am, the very heart of Britain, it seemed to say. So, watch your step, matey!

This slight sign of nervousness from his extremely dapper and usually cock-sure sergeant made Bishop, perversely, relax just a little. Myers was such an able social animal that to see him discomforted was almost worth the wear and tear on his own nerves.

His amusement, however, was short-lived. The moment he stepped into the final room, after a warren-like maze had led him to the east wing of the castle, he knew why they called it the Turner lounge. There were nothing but original, striking, if minor, Turners on every wall. Even he, who'd gained his knowledge of art from the Sunday newspaper supplements, knew priceless art when he saw it.

From a large pink sofa, a man rose slowly, and both policemen felt his aura of unassuming power immediately. He had a thin figure, offset by a large nose, and deep, penetrating eyes. In them, you could clearly see the bloodline of the Avonsleighs, and Bishop could well imagine this man, transplanted to the Battle of Waterloo, giving Napoleon some stick. Or the Battle of Hastings, fighting alongside the doomed Harold.

'The police, m'lord,' Meecham said, and then realized that he'd failed to get their names. He cast a stricken and apologetic look to the older man that he read at once. Both Myers and Bishop noticed it too, of course, and wondered what his lordship would do next.

He walked forward and held out his hand. Bishop hastily shook it. 'Inspector...?' George probed bluntly.

'Bishop, sir. This is Sergeant Myers.'

From his advantage of a few inches, Lord Avonsleigh looked down at the sergeant, one eyebrow slightly lifting.

He was a rather unusual figure for a policeman, George thought, in that he was dressed in a good quality suit, and wore a rather daringly coloured tie. His hair was jet black and brushed back in a rather foreign style, but his square, pugnacious face was so English it could have been stamped with the Union Jack.

'Well, I think you'd better come in, have some tea, and listen to what's been going on. Thank you, Meecham,' he said, gently dismissing his somewhat fazed butler. Meecham left, with rather a little more speed than was strictly dignified.

'My wife, Lady Avonsleigh, Colonel and Mrs Attling,' he said, glancing at the remaining three people in the room. Bishop nodded.

The colonel looked every inch the retired officer he undoubtedly was. No doubt he regretted not being born when India was still a part of the British Empire. His wife looked as if she lived constantly, but quite contentedly, in his shadow. One of those quaint Englishwomen who had surprising reserves of iron beneath the blue-rinsed hairdo and flowery summer frock.

Her ladyship was quite simply formidable. She looked alert, capable and totally at ease. Her chins quivered as she leaned forward and poured out two cups of suspiciously pale tea into exquisite china cups.

Bishop took a chair unhappily, wincing as it creaked under him. It had looked antique, and he only hoped it would hold. He was a large man, big-boned and heavy-set. He accepted the tea with a nervous start and an equally nervous smile as Lady Vee handed it over, and his nose twitched as the highly scented steam began rising from the cup. He knew it! One of those fancy, foul-tasting teas with an unpronounceable name.

He balanced the Royal Doulton cup in his massive hand, never intending to lift it to his lips. By his side, Myers drank with evident enjoyment. Since most of his salary went on clothes, he could rarely afford the rest of life's finer offerings, and he obviously intended to make the most of it when one came his way.

'Well, sir.… I mean, your lordship,' Bishop corrected himself quickly, trying to re-assert some sense of authority. It was not easy, surrounded by masterpieces and the silent, watchful company of his powerful audience. 'Perhaps you might explain, as concisely as possible, exactly what has happened?'

George nodded, but didn't speak for several seconds, obviously composing his thoughts. It was a good sign.

'Well, Inspector, it's really rather simple. Colonel Attling and his wife arrived for a visit just before three o'clock. As usual, we paused by the sunroom hall to admire the Munjib dagger, a rather fine example of Indian jewelled weaponry. The grandfather clock had just struck three. We all went onto the terrace, where we enjoyed a light tea in the sun and some general pleasantries. About half an hour later, we left the terrace and went back inside, the colonel and myself to play billiards, the ladies to…er…enjoy some conversation.'

He hasn't a clue what ladies get up to, Bishop thought with a tiny spark of amusement. His concentration, though, suffered not a whit, and he listened avidly as Lord Avonsleigh continued.

'As we walked into the small hall, we noticed that Meecham had suddenly stopped dead. It was…er…very unlike him.'

I'll bet, Bishop thought grimly.

'Naturally, we all looked to see what had upset him so, and followed his gaze to the dagger and saw for ourselves that, well, at the risk of sounding overly dramatic, we saw that it was dripping with blood.' He coughed, as if embarrassed by this statement. 'The clock then struck half past three, which made me, for one, almost jump out of my skin. I asked Meecham to make a thorough check of the castle. The rest of us went back to the sunroom to wait. Some minutes later—I can't say how long, I'm afraid—Meecham came back and informed me that Miss Simmons, my granddaughter's governess, was in the conservatory. Dead. I immediately ordered him to post one of the servants outside, to let no one in or out, and to touch nothing, and then inform the police.'

At this point he glanced at the colonel to see if he had missed anything out, but his old friend shook his head.

Bishop nodded. 'I see. Thank you, that's very clear. Perhaps you could tell us who else was in the castle at the time?'

Lord Avonsleigh nodded, already anticipating the question. By his side, Myers had been taking notes in competent shorthand, but now changed to longhand to write down the list of names.

'Of course. Well, there's my granddaughter, Lady Roberta, and her art tutor, Mr Malcolm Powell-Brooks. There was Meecham, of course, and his daughter Gayle, who is maid to her ladyship and also a tour guide here at the castle. Janice Beale, parlour maid, Elsie Bingham, kitchen maid, and our new cook, Miss Starling.'

By his side, Myers suddenly dropped his pencil.

Bishop, in particularly, looked suddenly sick. Both Avonsleigh and the colonel stared at the stricken policemen in some surprise.

'Miss Starling, did you say?' Bishop finally asked, his voice just managing to rise above a rasping, appalled whisper.

Lady Vee's eyes sharpened on the inspector.

'Yes, Inspector. Miss Starling,' his lordship confirmed briskly. 'Dashed if I know her first name. Do you, Vee, old gal?' He turned to his wife, aware of a slight loss of colour in her cheeks.

'Eh? Oh, no, I can't remember if it was mentioned on her references,' she murmured, her eyes never leaving the inspector's face. *Damn it all, don't say there was a problem with their cook as well*, she silently wailed to herself. That really would be too much.

'A small lady, is she?' Myers spoke for the first time, his voice hopeful.

Lord Avonsleigh snorted. 'Big as a horse, praise be. Fine figure of a woman, mind. Can't trust a skinny cook, I always say.' Then, aware of the dismayed look the two policemen exchanged, he moved very swiftly to the edge of his seat, his eyes narrowing. 'Why do you ask?' he demanded sharply.

Bishop managed a rather sickly smile. 'It's just that Miss Starling is rather well known in police circles, sir.'

'Good grief!' his lordship cried. 'You don't mean to say she did it?'

'Not our *cook*!' wailed Lady Vee forlornly, and so loudly, that both policemen jumped. Quite visibly.

'Oh, no, nothing like that,' Bishop hastened to reassure them, wondering what had suddenly set them off. And things had been going so well, too.

'I think you'd better explain yourself, Inspector,' his lordship said crisply, and Bishop felt his whole body snap to attention.

'Yes, sir. I mean, your lordship. Miss Starling has, at least twice in the past, er, helped police with their inquiries. That is, she has been instrumental in helping us solve several murders.'

'Several?' Lady Vee echoed, her chins wobbling alarmingly.

'Yes, my lady. Well, to my own certain knowledge, Miss Starling helped police officers to…er….' he trailed off, not quite sure how to put it.

'She solved the murders for you, you mean?' Vee cut through the waffle ruthlessly, and Bishop, defeated, mumbled something vaguely affirmative.

'Splendid,' Lady Vee breathed with relief, the awful feeling in the pit of her stomach happily subsiding. In fact, she positively beamed. The next instant, she reached for a bell rope and pulled, and Bishop cast his sergeant an anxious look.

Now what?

A moment later Meecham promptly appeared, was asked to fetch Miss Starling at once, and promptly disappeared again.

'What can you tell us about Miss Simmons, sir?' the Inspector asked, feeling a trickle of sweat run down his back. Murder at the castle was bad enough, but to have the infamous Jenny Starling in attendance as well. What had he done to deserve *that*?

He knew that his colleagues in Gloucester, namely an Inspector Mollineaux, thought very highly of the woman indeed, but he himself shared the view of the majority at his station. Amateurs were a pain in the—

'Well, she's only been with us about a month,' his lordship fortuitously interrupted his musings. 'Her first name's Ava, I believe. Her father owns the Giselle Gallery in Bicester; you may know it. She was brought in to teach Roberta, well, a little more refinement,' he explained. And the indulgent twinkle in his eye as he contemplated his wayward granddaughter left neither policeman in any doubt that the little girl was the apple of his eye. 'She was in her early thirties, I imagine. Quiet, competent. I liked her well enough. What else can I say?'

'Did she have a boyfriend?' Bishop probed delicately, but it was Lady Vee who answered. No doubt, because she knew that her husband wouldn't have had a clue.

'No, I don't think so, Inspector. She kept herself very much to herself. Not that she was unattractive, of course,' she added hastily. 'But if she had a sweetheart, she was very discreet about it.'

'I see,' the inspector said gloomily. In many cases where young women were killed, it was usually a man friend who was responsible. Jealous, or drunk, normally.

'Could anyone else have gained access to the castle, my lord? This afternoon, I mean?' Myers put in a question of his own.

Lord Avonsleigh scratched his head, and shrugged. 'I imagine so, Inspector. There's the gardening staff, and some of the local women who come in from the village to help Janice with the heavy work. We have tourists in, during the summer, so there's always lots of entrances and exits left open. But it's not a visitors' day today,' he added, making the policemen fairly wilt in relief. 'The doors are never locked during the day though, but even so, I rather doubt that anyone could have just wandered in, stabbed our governess and wandered out again, do you? Not without being seen by *somebody*.'

Bishop secretly agreed with him. Still, you couldn't rule anything out.

Just then there was a discreet tap on the door and Meecham walked in, followed by a tall woman with an extremely curvaceous figure who looked around with wary, but quite lovely, blue eyes.

Miss Jenny Starling herself.

Bishop felt his heart sink.

'Thank you, Meecham,' his lordship said, sensing his butler's heartfelt desire to flee.

He fled.

'Ah, Miss Starling.' Lady Vee beamed. 'Inspector Bishop here has just been telling us of your exploits.'

'Oh?' Jenny said warily. She knew that something was wrong. The kitchen had been deserted all afternoon. And there had been a strange atmosphere. As a consequence, her shoulders were quite tense. Now the police were here. What on earth was going on? And what had the police been telling Lady Vee, exactly? Nothing good, that was for sure, she thought, pursing her lips grimly.

'I'm afraid we've lost our governess, Miss Starling,' his lordship said, trying to break it to her gently.

Jenny blinked. Lost? Lost her where?

'Someone's killed her,' her ladyship added flatly, seeing the cook's rather puzzled look and knowing full well that gentleness was not required. Their new cook was obviously the kind of woman who could cope with almost anything.

Except, perhaps, a tart that refused to brown.

'Oh,' Jenny said flatly.

Ava Simmons, dead? All that waste! She'd been so young. Jenny bit back the sensation of anger and dismay that swamped her, and forced herself to look levelly at her employer.

'Exactly,' her ladyship continued crisply. 'And since you seem to be rather good at this sort of thing, I want you to accompany the inspector here wherever he goes, and lend a hand.'

Jenny gaped, then glanced across at the equally gobsmacked inspector. The inspector glared back. It would have been impossible to say which one of them looked the more dismayed.

'Oh,' Jenny said again. Even more flatly.

'It will help enormously to have a friendly face sitting in on all the questioning, don't you think, Inspector?' Lady Avonsleigh issued the challenge, obviously not expecting a fight.

'I expect so, my lady,' Bishop answered glumly, his lack of enthusiasm plain to one and all.

'That's settled then,' she said happily, steamrollering over him in classic style.

'Is there anything else we can do for you, Inspector?' Lord Avonsleigh asked, obviously not without sympathy for the policeman, and Bishop, relieved, put down his untouched cup of tea and rose.

'Not at the moment, sir, thank you. Perhaps I can speak to Meecham now?'

'Of course, of course. I dare say he's in the kitchen. Miss Starling will show you the way.'

Jenny obliged, very much aware of two pairs of hostile eyes boring into her broad back with every step she took. Not that she was worried about that, unduly, she had other things on her mind.

Ava Simmons dead. Killed. Murdered.

But who? And why?

IN THE KITCHEN, only Meecham and Elsie sat around the table. The butler half rose, then nervously sat back down again as the policemen came into the room. He looked pale, and the hands holding his tea cup shook.

Not a strong character, this, Bishop thought. A rather timid soul. But good at his job, he'd bet.

'Mr Meecham,' Bishop greeted him kindly. 'I'd like you to tell me exactly what you saw this afternoon.' He got the ball rolling immediately, nodding to Myers who was already poised, notebook handy. Both policemen sat opposite the butler, presenting a formidable show of force.

Meecham swallowed. Hard. 'Well, sir. I took the food out to the party on the terrace about, oh five past three, no later. And I returned just before half past to retrieve it.'

'Bit quick, weren't you?' Bishop asked, and Meecham flushed.

'They are hearty eaters, and the colonel has, well, a thing about food.'

'A thing?' Bishop repeated, surprised.

'Yes, sir.' But Meecham would not be drawn. He was, after all, still a butler. And discretion was his middle name.

'I see. Then what?'

'On our way out I noticed the dagger, sir. It was covered in blood: it was dripping down the wall.' The butler shuddered and took a hasty sip of hot tea, and Jenny found herself wishing she had a mug of her own.

Vividly now, she recalled the beautiful dagger to mind. And the fact that someone had used such a beautiful object to commit such an ugly act made her feel outraged. To be stabbed to death was awful.

Jenny, aware that she was in slight shock, briskly set about making herself a cup of strong, very sweet tea, at the same time keeping her ears firmly open as the police questioning continued. She knew from bitter experience that there would be many more hours of it to come yet, and she needed to keep her wits about her.

'You didn't notice it dripping in blood when you went to retrieve the tray, though?' Bishop asked sharply, pointing out the inconsistency with a sharply suspicious tone.

Meecham paled further. 'Er...no, sir, I didn't. I don't suppose I looked.'

'But you *did* on the way out,' Bishop pressed suspiciously. 'When the others were with you?'

Meecham nodded miserably. 'Yes, sir. I did. I don't know what made me look up at it. Probably because I knew the colonel was behind me, and I remembered how he admired it so.'

'Hmm,' Bishop made no comment. In truth, he was not *all* that suspicious of Meecham. (God forbid, the butler did it: he'd never live it down back at the police station.) But he would have to go and see this dagger before the forensic boys took samples.

He was very curious to see it for himself *in situ*. 'What next?'

'His lordship asked me to check on the staff, sir. To see if anyone was missing. I knew that Janice was out, sir, as it was her afternoon off. And I could hear Lady Roberta in the music-room. She was playing the piano, so I went there first. I expected Miss Simmons to be there too, but it was Mr Powell-Brooks, the art tutor, who was taking her for the piano lesson.'

'Was that unusual?'

'No, sir. Mr Powell-Brooks is quite an accomplished pianist. He sometimes took a lesson, if Miss Simmons was ill, or a little late in turning up.'

Jenny frowned, and glanced across her cup. Surely Ava Simmons was not the kind to be late? And since she'd only been here a month, she'd still be anxious about her time keeping. Why wouldn't Meecham or Powell-Brooks have realized the same thing? Or perhaps they had.

'I see. Then where did you go?'

'Here, sir.'

'That's right, Inspector, I remember.' Jenny spoke to

him directly for the first time. 'Mr. Meecham opened the door and glanced in. I remember that he looked rather pale and distracted. I can't say what time that was, exactly, though.'

'And you were here alone?' Bishop asked her harshly, and with an abruptness that was most definitely rude.

'With Elsie,' Jenny corrected him gently, getting in her alibi first, before he had a chance to ask her for it.

Bishop glanced at the kitchen maid, who raised her chin and stared at him like a dog that was getting ready to bite.

'I see,' Bishop said, backing off. Very wisely, Jenny thought.

'And then?' He turned back to Meecham.

'I knew my daughter was in her ladyship's bedroom, sir, getting her bath ready.'

So soon in the afternoon, Jenny thought in some surprise, then gave a mental shrug. Since she wasn't familiar with Lady Vee's ablutions, she supposed it could be a fair statement. And if Meecham wanted to leave his daughter out of it as much as possible, it was probably only natural.

'So only the governess was unaccounted for,' Bishop said. 'What made you go straight to the conservatory?' he asked quickly.

Meecham jumped. 'I didn't, sir. I went to her room first, but no one answered my knocking. I searched several rooms before noticing that the conservatory door was standing open. Since the gardener was most insistent it should always be kept shut, I naturally went to see, and there she was.'

'How was she lying?'

'On her back, sir.'

'What was she wearing?'

Meecham blinked. 'Er, I don't think I noticed, sir.'

Bishop nodded. Probably hadn't, poor beggar. Shouldn't wonder if he didn't pass out for a few moments. He looked the type. 'I see. Thank you, Meecham. If you could just show me where the dagger is hanging, that will be all for the moment.'

In spite of Lady Vee's obvious wishes that she dog the inspector's footsteps, and thus keep her informed, the cook made no move to rise and follow them.

Bishop noticed and audibly sighed with relief, and quickly followed the trembling butler out of the kitchen before she could change her mind.

'So she's dead then.'

The flat, abrupt voice belonged to Elsie, and Jenny glanced at her. 'Seems so,' she agreed quietly. The kitchen maid nodded and reached for her cup. Her gnarled hands, Jenny noticed without surprise, were shaking.

Looking up quickly, the cook saw an expression, so fleeting it was almost impossible to pinpoint, flash across the maid's morose face. But her next words were prosaic enough.

'There'll be hell to pay, I expect,' Elsie said glumly.

Jenny sighed, remembering the policeman's hostile but resigned expression when Lady Avonsleigh had all but demanded that the cook be kept informed.

'I daresay there will be,' she agreed.

She felt suddenly tired. Ava Simmons was dead. And

someone in this castle, this afternoon, had killed her. And her ladyship wanted her to find out who did it. Was it just because Lady Vee didn't have confidence in the police? Or, more likely, did she just want a friendly eye and ear in the police camp?

Or, Jenny thought with a sickening lurch in her stomach, was she worried about what the police might discover?

SIX

Bishop stared at the dagger, fascinated in spite of himself. The dagger handle was relatively clean, and gleamed in small pinpoints of jewellike light—deep red, emerald green and gold. In contrast, the blade was covered in drying blood. On the white wall, the trickles of blood that had run from it were turning into rusty stains that chilled his own blood and sent shivers up his spine. No doubt about it, he mused—it was a macabre sight.

'Better get the forensic lads over here when they've finished,' Bishop said, speaking his thoughts out loud. Not that he expected them to find any fingerprints on the handle. 'Right, Meecham. The conservatory,' Bishop dragged his eyes away from the Munjib dagger, and glanced at the butler, who was going slightly green around the gills.

Meecham left with alacrity, only to slow down and come to a dead stop just a few yards from the conservatory. Taking his dismissal for granted, he then left quickly. If either policeman had been paying more attention, they might have wondered if there was more to his actions than mere squeamishness.

Almost blindly, Meecham moved quickly down the corridor. He had to reach Gayle. He had to ask her to run to the gatehouse, quick. It might not be too late.

'The doc's here,' Bishop muttered, watching the police surgeon as he bent over the body, inspecting methodically but touching very little. 'Must have arrived not long after we did.' For several moments the two policemen watched the team at work—the forensic people examining in minute detail the flagged stone floor of the conservatory, the doctor in attendance on the corpse.

Even in death, Ava Simmons had managed to retain her dignity. Her skirt had risen slightly, but still covered her knees decorously. Her lips were closed, not gaping open, as was the case of so many corpses Bishop had seen over the years. Her eyes were closed, as if asleep. Even her hair was mostly still neatly in place. Only her blouse marred the picture of gentility. Over the region of her heart was a bright red patch that had leaked onto the floor. It looked so out of place on the otherwise meticulous governess that Bishop had to look away.

The doctor looked up, saw them, and rose slowly. 'Inspector Bishop. You bagged this one then?' he asked jovially.

Bishop nodded sourly. 'Myers, take one of the lab boys to that little dagger, would you?' He himself was not sure he could find the way back, but he knew Myers had all the instincts of a homing pigeon.

'What can you tell me?' Bishop asked when the others had left, already knowing that it would not be much. MEs were notoriously tight-mouthed when it came to putting their reputations on the line.

'The body's still slightly warm to the touch,' the doctor said, and glanced at his watch. 'It's nearly five now, so I would say she's been dead not more than four hours, not less than one. Given that this room is so warm anyway. But don't quote me.'

Bishop nodded. 'We've got it narrowed down to between three o'clock and three-thirty.'

The doctor nodded. It fitted. 'Death due to a single stab wound to the heart, as far as I can tell,' he continued, the usual caution now creeping into his voice. 'Death would have been practically instantaneous, I would have thought. But don't—'

'I know, I know. Don't quote you.' Bishop sighed and looked around at the shelves of plants still neatly standing side by side, and the undisturbed stack of pots on the floor not far from the body. 'She didn't put up much of a struggle,' he noted sadly.

The doctor shrugged. 'She probably wasn't given the chance. The wound was caused by a long, very thin and sharp-pointed blade. Slightly rounded, I would have said. Unusual.'

Bishop nodded. 'There's a dagger, covered in blood, coming our way. It fits the description.'

The doctor sighed, looking down at her. 'A woman in the prime of her life, Inspector. She looks a nice sort.'

Bishop nodded. Ava Simmons *did* look a nice sort. Not the kind that usually ended up murdered.

'Bit of a feather in your cap, this case, isn't it?' the doctor asked, and Bishop snorted. He was saved from answering by the return of Myers, the dagger enclosed in an evidence bag, which he handed over to the doctor. Nobody expected that the blood would not match that of the victim. Or the blade, that of the knife wound.

'Well, I suppose we'd better get on with it,' Bishop said. 'I want another word with our delightful Miss Starling.'

At the mention of the name, the doctor looked up in surprise, then grinned at the morose expression on the inspector's face. Even the pathologists had begun to hear of the growing fame of Jenny Starling. The last of the great amateur detectives, no less.

Wisely though, he said nothing, but Myers winked at him behind his inspector's back as the two men left.

JENNY LOOKED UP in surprise as Meecham all but rushed into the kitchen and came to sudden halt. He looked around in surprise. 'Is Gayle not here?' he asked, slightly out of breath.

Jenny shook her head, her eyes curious. 'Obviously not,' she said softly. 'Is something wrong, Mr Meecham?'

Meecham flushed, suddenly aware that he was acting strangely. 'Er, no. I thought that she was in her ladyship's rooms but she's not. Nor is she in her own room. I was, er—' He broke off as the door opened and his daughter walked in. 'There you are. Gayle, we have to, er….' He glanced back over his shoulder and moved further away.

Jenny headed for the oven, her ears pricked. In spite of that, she caught only the odd word or two. 'Gatehouse', she was sure was one of them. And 'must intercept' another. Even whispering, Meecham sounded distraught.

Over the cover of a saucepan lid, the cook looked

across at father and daughter, and saw Gayle lay a calming hand on her father's arm. Very briefly she shook her head, and although Jenny never heard her, could lip-read the two words clearly. 'Too late.'

Meecham's shoulders drooped and he trudged wearily back to the centre of the kitchen, slumping down at the table.

Elsie, moving in that unerringly silent manner of hers, quickly placed a steaming hot cup of tea in front of him. Jenny was not the only one in that kitchen with sharp eyes and ears, apparently. A moment later, the door opened again, and this time the two policemen walked in. Bishop glanced at her, then saw Gayle, and paused.

'Ah, Miss Meecham,' Bishop gave her his best 'kindly uncle' smile and indicated a chair. Gayle gave him a single, blank-eyed look, and sat down. Myers moved opposite, pulling out his notebook. Jenny didn't miss the flash of fear in Gayle's dark eyes. Nevertheless, she folded steady hands in her lap, and waited patiently. There was something both stoic and tense about her.

Bishop leaned back in his own chair, making it squeak. 'As you can imagine, Miss Meecham, we have to ask everybody in the castle where they were this afternoon and what they might have seen or heard. Also, of course, any other thing they may need to tell us. Nobody likes to speak ill of the dead, I know, but often the only clue to someone's murder lies in the personality of the murder victim herself. You understand?' Bishop asked, surprising Jenny considerably.

She hadn't thought that Bishop had so much finesse,

let alone understanding. Subconsciously, she began to relax. Ava Simmons was in good hands.

'Yes, Inspector. I shall do whatever I can to help, of course,' Gayle said coolly. If Bishop had hoped to win her over, it was very apparent that he hadn't succeeded.

'Can you tell me where you were from three o'clock to half past three this afternoon, Gayle?' Bishop asked briskly, cutting out the soft flannel now, since it was obviously wasted on her.

'I was in her ladyship's bedroom. I was getting her bath ready.'

'For half an hour?' Bishop asked, his scepticism rife.

'The towels have to be heated, Inspector. Her ladyship's change of clothes pressed. The soap, talc, bath salts and shampoo, all have to be retrieved, opened, and co-ordinated. Her ladyship's rollers have to be heated... really, Inspector, must I go into the *intimate* details of Lady Vee's toilette?'

Good for you, Jenny thought with a quickly suppressed grin, seeing a dull red flush creep over Bishop's thick, bullish neck. He hastily backtracked, hideously embarrassed.

It was a perfect blind, and the cook knew it. Perhaps Gayle really *had* been doing all that she said she had. But if she hadn't, she'd certainly made sure Bishop wouldn't keep harping on about it.

Jenny's eyes narrowed on Gayle's calm face. She really was a very competent girl. Very able. A very good liar, perhaps.

'And you were alone?' Bishop pressed, recovering his equilibrium somewhat.

'No. Father was in the next room. His lordship's dressing-room.'

'Oh?' Bishop turned to Meecham.

'Yes, Inspector. After delivering the tea tray, I knew I would not be needed for a while. I had Lord Avonsleigh's smoking jacket to sponge—he likes a cigar before dinner.'

'You were concerned about his smoking jacket at three o'clock in the afternoon?' Bishop asked, his voice dripping with open disbelief now.

'I said it needed to be sponged, Inspector. As you know, velvet takes a long time to dry,' Meecham responded, trying not to underline the inspector's ignorance too much. It didn't do to alienate the police.

Bishop sighed deeply, obviously feeling out of place in this world of lords and ladies, smoking jackets and butlers. Jenny almost felt sorry for him.

'I see. But either one of you could have left the room any time without the other seeing?'

'We talked all the time,' Gayle said quietly. 'If one of us had failed to answer, well, we would only have to take a few steps to reach the next room. Father left just before three-thirty to take back the tea tray. I continued with the bath, until it was obvious that the guests were staying longer than predicted. I then left, and met my father in the hall a short while later. He told me about Miss Simmons.'

'I see,' Bishop said flatly. So father and daughter were alibiing each other. It was not totally unexpected, but it left him no further forward. It could all have been as they said. Maybe.

Bishop turned reluctantly to the cook. 'And you, Miss Starling? Where were you?'

'I was here the whole time, Inspector, as I said before. First, preparing the tea tray, then, afterwards, the evening meal. Which reminds me....' She got up to check that Elsie had peeled the potatoes.

'And you never left the kitchen once?' Bishop asked sharply. He could almost wish that *she* had done it. That would remove a thorn from many a policeman's side.

'No, I didn't,' Jenny said shortly, accurately reading his thoughts. Damned cheek!

Bishop turned to the ferocious-looking kitchen maid with conspicuous courage. 'And you are Miss Bingham?' Bishop pulled her name from the depths of his rather good memory.

'I was here too,' Elsie said quickly, her voice gruff and challenging. 'All afternoon.'

Hearing this blatant lie, Jenny paused in the act of filling the vast saucepans with water. She looked over her shoulder, her eyes colliding with that of the inspector. Jenny sighed.

'That's not quite true, Elsie,' she pointed out, as casually as she could manage. 'I did ask you to go down to the cellar for some flour and swedes. Remember?'

Elsie scowled, but nodded. 'Oh. Ah, so you did,' she owned. She didn't look particularly put out or particularly defensive. She sounded as if she'd just forgotten the incident.

'What time was this?' Bishop asked quickly, and the two women exchanged a long, measured look.

'About quarter past three, I think,' Jenny admitted reluctantly.

'How long did it take you, Elsie?' Bishop asked, and saw the old girl's head swing back sharply in his direction. Her eyes were as hard as a hawk's.

'A few minutes, I expect,' Elsie said. 'The cellars are right dark, and them steps are dead steep. I took me time. I'll show you if you like.'

Bishop nodded to Myers. The instructions were unspoken, but plain to everyone in the room. *See where the cellar is in relation to the conservatory. Time your movements. See if the old girl could have done the killing, retrieved the foodstuffs and come back all within a few minutes.*

Jenny watched them go, her eyes troubled. She glanced back to Bishop, and with the potatoes ready to go, returned to her seat. Things were moving too fast. She needed to slow them down and to start thinking.

'Would it have taken long, do you think, Inspector?' she asked the first of many questions that would need to be answered. 'The actual killing, I mean?'

Bishop shook his head. 'No. It was a single blow. She wasn't expecting it. She didn't struggle. It could have taken less than a minute.' Now that he had accepted the inevitability of Miss Starling's involvement, he was finding it surprisingly easy to talk to her. Like several police officers before him, he was beginning to suspect a sharp intelligence at work under that rather startling exterior. She might look like a surprisingly lovely, statuesque cook, Bishop thought, but she'd got a mind like a steel trap.

Jenny nodded. 'I see,' she said heavily. Poor Ava.
She couldn't have known much about it. There was at
least that blessing.

Just then, the door was flung open and Roberta
bounded into the room. She looked like a wild thing,
her hair flying and her eyes red from weeping. She
headed straight for Jenny, homing in for comfort.

'It isn't true, is it?' Roberta gasped, wiping her
cheeks with the back of her hand and sniffling loudly.
All traces of the cocky teenager were gone, and she was,
temporarily at least, still little more than a child, suddenly confronted with one of the harsher facts of life.
Unfair, sudden, and ugly death.

'I'm afraid it is, Lady Roberta,' Jenny said gently.

'I don't believe it. It can't be true. I *didn't like her*!'
Roberta wailed, making perfect sense to the cook, but
startling Bishop into sitting forward and taking a sudden, intense notice.

'I know,' Jenny said soothingly. 'When someone dies
that you don't much like, it seems worse somehow. You
feel guilty that you didn't like them better. You wished
you'd made friends.'

'That's it exactly. Oh, Miss Starling, you *do* understand,' Roberta said, relieved. 'I really couldn't believe
it when Gramps told me,' she carried on, sniffing even
more loudly.

Jenny reached into her voluminous apron and ex-
tracted a hankie. Roberta used it robustly. 'It's absolutely awful,' she said at last. 'Something has to be
done. They can't get away with it. Whoever did it, they

have to pay, Miss Starling,' she said, with all the vehemence of the young.

Jenny nodded. 'Whoever did it will be caught,' she said grimly. 'I promise.'

'So do I,' said Bishop, his deep voice making Roberta jump. She looked around, blushed, and quickly stood nervously to one side, putting her hands behind her back.

'Oh. Hello. You must be a policeman,' she said, with touching aplomb.

Bishop smiled warmly. Not even he was immune to girlish charm, it seemed. 'Indeed I am. And I'm glad to hear you say what you just did. I just know you'll be a great help in finding Miss Simmons' killer.'

Roberta beamed, and Bishop beamed back.

He has a daughter of his own around about her age, Jenny realized in a sudden flash of intuition. Well, well.

'I will, if I can,' Roberta added, with an anxious frown.

'But what can I do?' she added eagerly.

'Well, for a start, you could tell me where you were between three o'clock and half past this afternoon. That would be a great help.'

'Oh, that's easy,' Roberta said, a little disappointed by the banality of the question. Now that the shock was wearing off, the resilience of the young was taking its place. Now she was excited. Keen for the adventure to begin.

And Jenny felt a sudden stab of fear.

She was so young. Too eager. Which meant she was vulnerable. What if she actually found something out?

With her insatiable curiosity, it could lead to all sorts of trouble.

'I was in the music room playing the piano with Malc.'

'Malc? Oh, Mr Powell-Brooks.'

'That's right. We got there about, oh, ten to three, and we were still playing when Gramps came to tell us why Simm hadn't shown up.'

Bishop followed this breathless explanation with ease.

'So she was supposed to take you for piano?' he clarified.

'Hmm. But Malc can play just as well as she can,' Roberta said with a cheeky grin. And she much preferred him to teach her too, she added silently.

'And you never left the music-room? You or Malc, er, Mr Powell-Brooks?'

Roberta shook her head.

Bishop nodded. 'I see. Tell me about Miss Simmons,' he began, but was interrupted by the return of Elsie and Myers. The sergeant gave his superior a meaningful look, but neither spoke. Jenny vowed to find the food cellar the first chance she got, but she already knew, with a sinking heart, that it would turn out to be not far from the conservatory.

'Can anyone tell me anything about the dagger used to kill Miss Simmons?' Bishop asked, looking around without much hope.

Obviously there was no point in trying to keep the identity of the murder weapon a secret—not when so many had seen it covered with blood. 'Had it ever gone missing before? Did anyone see anybody else taking unusual notice of it?'

Jenny, in the act of raising a cup of tea to her lips, suddenly stopped. Instantly Bishop's eyes fixed on hers.

The cook was remembering her call to the butler's pantry, and she glanced guiltily at Meecham. At the same moment, Meecham remembered what he had been doing, only an hour before Ava Simmons was killed.

He looked at the inspector, going deathly pale.

'I didn't kill her,' he said weakly, and Jenny felt like kicking him sharply under cover of the table. Didn't he realize how guilty he sounded? Gayle obviously did. She gave her father a stricken look, and Jenny felt her mouth go suddenly dry.

She thinks he may have done it, Jenny realized, in a sudden flash of intuitive understanding. But why?

SEVEN

BISHOP TRIED TO keep a rising sense of excitement firmly in check as he stared at the butler impassively.

'I hadn't realized that anyone *had* accused you of the murder, Mr Meecham,' he said mildly. And Jenny, sensing instinctively that Inspector Bishop was at his most dangerous when appearing to be at his most reasonable, found herself stepping in where angels would, at the very least, have thought twice about treading.

'I think, Inspector, that Mr Meecham is worried that because he was the last person to handle the dagger, it might make him the prime suspect,' Jenny explained, her cool and reasonable tones dripping into the tense air like soothing ointment. 'Which is, of course, ridiculous,' she added softly, just for good measure.

Out of the corner of her eye she saw Meecham cast beseeching eyes in her direction. Bishop, on the other hand, turned gimlet eyes her way. 'Oh yes, Miss Starling? And just how do you happen to know this?' he demanded.

'Because I saw him cleaning it, of course,' Jenny said simply, taking the wind out of his sails with no effort at all.

'Oh?' Bishop turned back to the quivering Meecham.

'Well, yes,' Meecham said. 'Of course I was the last

to handle it. Nobody else would have any business even touching it.'

'You are the one who cleans it?' Bishop asked gently, one bushy eyebrow disappearing into his hairline.

Meecham gulped. 'Yes, Inspector. You see, I knew that the colonel was visiting today, and whenever the colonel visits, he always wants to see the dagger. That's why the family always entertain in a room that leads past the dagger, so that the colonel doesn't have to actually ask to be shown it. They're very consid—'

'Yes, yes,' Bishop interrupted, feeling the excitement beginning to abate. Drat that cook. Giving the butler confidence just when he needed to be kept off-balance. He cast Jenny a fulminating gaze, which was totally wasted on her. She merely glanced placidly back at him, her lovely blue eyes making him uncomfortably aware of her sex appeal.

'But what has that to do with you being the last to handle the dagger, Meecham?' Myers, seeing that his superior was distracted, quickly leapt in, keeping up the pressure.

Meecham turned bewildered eyes in the dapper sergeant's direction.

'Well, I had to clean it, of course,' Meecham said, puzzlement plain in his voice. 'Whenever the colonel comes, I always clean the Munjib dagger,' he explained, as if talking to a particularly backward infant. 'I am the butler,' he informed them imperiously, his tones beginning to ring with indignation. 'It's my job to ensure that everything runs smoothly when they're entertaining. Why, if the colonel saw the dagger in anything but a spotless condition, his lordship would be mortified. He'd be—'

'Enough!' Bishop roared, holding up a huge hand and winning instant silence. For a moment he closed his eyes, then he took a deep breath, his massive shoulders heaving up and down. Then he opened his eyes once more. He turned to Meecham, his voice so sweet and reasonable that Jenny had to turn away to hide her smile.

'I understand, Meecham, that you cleaned the dagger. That you always clean the dagger when the colonel comes. That you take it as your life's work to keep the blasted dagger spotless,' his voice was beginning to rise again. Realizing it, he smiled and lowered his tone once more. Ever-so-sweetly, so that it made the cavities in your teeth positively ache, he added quietly, 'Can you tell me when?'

'When?' Meecham echoed, overawed by the display.

'Yes,' Bishop gritted through teeth that would surely be worn to a nub if he carried on grinding them in the way that he was doing. 'When. At what time was the dagger taken down from its usual place, and when did you put it back?'

'Er, it would have been about half past two when I finished and put it back. I'd been at it for at least an hour. It's hard to get between the gems without....' Meecham quickly trailed off when the inspector's eyes closed and the shoulders heaved once more.

'Thank you. I see.' Bishop rose and beckoned to his sergeant, then left. He wasn't particularly sure where he was going. He only knew that he wanted to get out of that kitchen before he found himself tearing out great chunks of his hair—which he could ill afford to lose.

'Not very helpful that, sir,' Myers said diplomatically.

'No. Let's see what the gardeners have to say. I want to take a look at that conservatory from the outside.'

That sounded reasonable enough, Bishop thought. And he needed some fresh air. It was going to be a long, long day.

Myers's lips twitched, but he made no comment. Myers was nobody's fool.

JENNY WAS RELIEVED to see that Meecham was finally regaining his equilibrium. At 7.30 on the dot, Jenny loaded the tray with steak and kidney pie, mashed potatoes, diced swede and carrots, and watched Meecham go away with it, straight-backed and dignified. As Elsie saw to the others, Jenny wondered exactly why she had come to Meecham's rescue so swiftly.

Oh, she liked him, right enough. And felt sorry for him. And yet, for all she knew, Meecham *might* have killed Ava Simmons. Or Meecham and Gayle together. That sounded rather more likely. Meecham was not exactly made of iron, whereas Gayle....

But was that fair to Gayle?

She hated how murder brought out every suspicious inch of her normally sweet nature. She sighed, and checked the rhubarb for acidity. It tingled against her inner cheeks perfectly. At least something was going right today. As she turned, she glanced around the despondent diners at the table, realizing that someone besides poor Ava was missing.

Of course, Janice! It was her afternoon off.

They were a quiet bunch that evening. Malcolm-Powell-Brooks found himself wishing that Roberta were present. She could be a little pain, sometimes, and her crush on him a bit embarrassing, but he'd have welcomed her chatter and youth with open arms. His nerves were like violin strings. Elsie, opposite him, seemed to be pushing her food around her plate in a manner that was guaranteed to irk Jenny no end. Gayle ate almost defiantly, the cook thought, with some worry. This girl feels guilty about something, Jenny was sure of that. But what possible motive could Gayle have for killing Ava? What motive could any of them have for that matter?

'Pass the salt please,' Malcolm said, to no one in particular, just to break the silence. Elsie obliged. Meecham returned. Jenny watched him sit down and stare at his food. He didn't even bother to so much as pick up his fork.

'Oh really, this is ridiculous,' Jenny snapped, making everyone jump. 'We might just as well get it all over with, and talk about it,' she carried on briskly, only to jump out of her own skin when a soft voice suddenly asked from a gloomy corner of the kitchen, 'Talk about what?'

The whole table turned around, white-faced and round-eyed. But the female voice belonged not to the vengeful, accusing ghost of Ava Simmons, but to a rather puzzled-looking Janice. She had just entered through the side-door leading from the garden, and was walking forward with a determinedly jaunty step.

'Didn't get to have any dinner after all,' she chirped.

'Danny was supposed to take me to the fish and chip shop, but....' Her cheerful chatter trailed off as everyone continued to stare at her blankly. 'What's up? Don't say you've eaten it all,' she laughed, but her laughter was hollow, and her eyes flitted about restlessly.

Jenny quickly ladled out the last morsels of the staff pie onto a plate and piled it high with vegetables. 'Sit down, Janice,' she said softly, and waited until she'd done so.

'What's up, for Pete's sake,' the chambermaid wailed, giving another hollow laugh. 'It's like a morgue in here.'

Her choice of words couldn't have been worse. Beside her, Elsie snorted. ''Tis. Just like it, my girl. Someone's killed her.'

Janice paled. 'Killed who?' she squeaked, then, for the first time, noticed the empty seat. 'You mean Ava?' she whispered, looking straight at Jenny for confirmation.

'Eat your dinner,' Jenny said flatly.

'But...what happened?'

'Someone stabbed her,' Elsie said bluntly. 'With that fancy Indian dagger of his nibs's. In the conservatory, they say. Anyway, she's dead, and that's that.'

And with that, Elsie took a determined bite of steak.

'We're sorry, Janice, to have it blurted out like that,' Gayle said, giving Elsie a reproving look. 'It's a bit of a shock, I know.'

Jenny barely heard Gayle's soothing words to Janice, who had started to weep quietly over her plate. She was still staring at Elsie. That the kitchen maid had been brutally blunt was not in question: it was the fact that she had been *so* brutal that held Jenny's attention.

It had always been her opinion that people who came out with callous statements in times of tragedy did so not necessarily because of a lack of feeling, but more often than not in a vain attempt to cover up deeper feelings. Without any evidence save her own instinct, she was sure that Elsie, placidly mashing gravy into her potatoes, was in the grip of some strong emotion.

But what? Fear? Grief? Anger?

'Oh, how terrible!' Janice wailed at last. 'I can't believe it!'

'I'm afraid the police will want a word, Janice,' Malcolm Powell-Brooks interrupted her, running a harassed hand through his hair.

Jenny glanced at him, aware that the only occasions she'd seen him without his habitual artists' smock were at mealtimes. Although it was never as paint-smeared as Lady Roberta's, it did tend to cover him like a tent, with voluminous pockets and loose sleeves. Now, dressed for dinner, Jenny could quite see why Lady Roberta was so star-struck, for he looked exceedingly handsome in his lightweight blue suit. Especially tonight, when shock had made him paler than ever, lending him the air of a Shakespearean tragic hero.

'I don't know anything,' Janice said quickly, interrupting Jenny's musings. 'Why should the police want to talk to me?' she added defensively. 'I wasn't even here.'

Meecham, who had obviously not been listening, but had been off in a world of his own, suddenly rose and glanced tellingly at the clock. Jenny jumped up and ladled piping hot rhubarb into a beautiful desert bowl, and gave the custard a final re-heating. It was creamy and pale, and just a little sweeter than usual. But for once, the cook's thoughts were on other matters. And it took something very momentous indeed to take Jenny Starling's mind off food. Especially a decent custard.

'Janice, what time did you leave, exactly?' she asked, taking the rest of the desert to the table and feeling not at all offended that nobody rushed to ladle out some helpings.

Janice gave her an odd look, and the cook smiled beguilingly. 'It's just that the police are bound to ask, and sometimes you can get so confused if you haven't got things straight in your mind first,' Jenny wheedled craftily.

'Oh. Yes, I suppose so,' Janice said, her pretty blonde brows furrowing in concentration. 'Well it must have been, I don't know, a quarter to two when I left here.' She didn't sound very sure, but Jenny put that down to her rather vague nature. Some people were just naturally not very well-organized.

'And where did you go?' the cook persisted casually, reaching for the rhubarb.

'To meet Danny, of course,' Janice sounded surprised. 'We had arranged to meet at the bottom of the hill, so I took the shortcut through Seth's precious vegetable garden and down the old footpath. You know.'

Jenny didn't know, since she'd not yet had time to even explore the castle properly, let alone the surrounding village, but it all sounded reasonable enough.

'Why didn't Danny come up to the castle?' Malcolm asked, just a little of his old mischievous self breaking through.

Janice gave him a fulminating glance. 'Like I just said, I'd already arranged to meet him at the bottom of the hill, that's why,' she said waspishly.

Didn't want him hanging around Ava, more like, Jenny thought accurately. She'd seen for herself the way Danny had been trying to worm his way into the governess's favour.

Which was odd that, when you thought about it.

'And did you?' Jenny asked, firmly keeping her mind on the matters at hand. 'Meet him there, I mean?'

Janice glanced at her quickly. 'Why do you ask?' she challenged defensively, only now realizing how cleverly the cook was grilling her.

Jenny shrugged her shoulders nonchalantly. 'It's just that the police are bound to ask you, that's all.'

'You see, Danny would be your alibi, dear heart,' Malcolm said helpfully.

'Oh, I get it,' Janice said miserably.

Something's wrong, Jenny thought astutely, and sighed heavily. She had hoped that at least one person could be eliminated from the list of suspects, and Janice, being the only one not here this afternoon, had looked like the ideal candidate for being in the free and clear. Now, though even that looked unlikely.

Meecham returned, empty dishes bearing mute testimony that at least the family's appetites continued unabated. And why shouldn't they, Jenny thought, with just a pinch of asperity. They were the only ones who didn't have a possible murder charge hanging over their heads.

Nobody suspected them, after all. Unless…Jenny paled slightly. Oh no. Don't go there! Firmly, she turned her thoughts back to Janice. 'So, was Danny waiting for you?' she prompted, and Janice bit her lip unhappily.

She shook her head reluctantly. 'No. He stood me up, didn't he.'

'Oh hell,' Jenny said, with feeling. 'Did you go straight into the village? Were you seen?'

'Oh yes,' Janice said eagerly. Too eagerly.

By her side, Meecham paused in the act of pouring out some custard. He glanced quickly at Janice, then away again.

'What did you do then?' Jenny prompted. Really, she thought crossly. This was like trying to pull teeth.

'Oh, not much. Took the bus into Banbury. Did a bit of shopping. Saw a film.'

'Which one?' Jenny asked quickly, and even more quickly added off-handedly, 'If it was any good, I might take a look myself.'

'Oh it was some sort of weepy,' Janice said quickly, then frowned. 'You know, one of those sugary-sweet American ones? Thing is, I can't quite remember what it was called.'

'And you never returned to the castle? When Danny didn't show up?'

Janice vehemently shook her head, and again Meecham stared at her, then turned away abruptly. But by then Jenny had already gone to the stove and so missed the butler's sharp glance.

The cook's thoughts were elsewhere anyway. Janice had been stood up. Danny had failed to show. Where had he been instead?

'I think, Janice,' Jenny said, beginning to stack the dishes, 'that you should find the police and tell them the truth. There's an Inspector Bishop and a Sergeant Myers about somewhere. I'm sure they haven't left. I should go and see them and get it over with, if I were you.'

She returned to the table, noting that Janice couldn't quite meet her eyes. 'It would be better if you sought them out and offered your own story, rather than wait for them to come to you. It might look a bit odd, otherwise,' she added quietly, sure that the maid had got the message by now.

Jenny sat down and then promptly shot back up again, with just a small 'yip' of surprise. Startled, everyone half-rose, varying looks of panic on their faces as they stared towards the cook.

Jenny, though, had not been stabbed.

Staring down at her chair and rubbing her ample bottom, that was tingling unhappily, she reached forward and lifted Henry from her chair, holding the tortoise aloft and scowling at the aloof-looking reptile.

'How the dickens did this creature climb onto my chair?' she asked breathlessly. If the circumstances had been different, she might have believed one of her fellow dinners had put him there deliberately as a practical joke.

The tortoise certainly got about for such a cumbersome animal.

Elsie was the first to break out into laughter, which

immediately set everyone else off. Jenny held Henry out in front of her as if he had leprosy, and laughed the hardest of them all.

Naturally, just because they were all laughing like loons, Inspector Bishop chose just that moment to walk into the room.

EIGHT

INSPECTOR BISHOP CAME back the next morning at 7.30, having slept like a log. He must have woken up like one too, for, as he walked into the castle's warm kitchen, his face was wooden, and he was walking in a particularly stiff manner. He'd come to keep Miss Starling 'appraised'.

He'd had a phone call at his house late last night from the chief constable himself who'd told him to get this case solved fast. But word was now rife in the village. Already, he could feel them banding together. Who knew what clues were being buried? What alibis were being sharpened up? If the killer were local and popular, it would make his life practically unbearable.

Jenny took in the policeman's misery with one all-seeing glance and took a plate from the hotplate. She herself had been up since six, unable to sleep, her mind going in circles. Although it was true that she had helped the police in the past, she'd never been caught up in anything quite like this. For a start, nobody at the castle appeared to have a *motive* for killing Ava Simmons. At least, none that she knew of. But then, she was a stranger here. She didn't know these people well. The castle might be teeming with all sorts of secrets that she had no way of tapping into. And yet, she must. She didn't like murder. And she certainly didn't approve of people getting away with it.

She carefully lifted three sizzling sausages, two rashers of thick bacon, two fried eggs, tomatoes and fried bread from the pan and transferred them to the plate.

Where to start? Ava Simmons, respectable woman, middle-class, well educated and perfectly pleasant, just wasn't your average murder victim. So why was she dead?

Bishop, who'd come away from home on a piece of toast and a boiled egg, watched the approaching plate with acute envy. That envy turned to astonished delight when the cook put it in front of him. 'There'll be toast and marmalade to follow, Inspector,' she said mildly, and poured herself a cup of tea. 'I've already eaten,' she added, a definite twinkle in her eye. She hadn't, but she wanted to get the inspector into a good mood.

'So, I expect you've questioned all the cleaners from the village and checked their alibis? And the gardeners?' she began, so conversationally, that Bishop, tucking into a succulent sausage, nodded his head without even thinking about it.

'I did, but no dice.' Bishop waved a fork smeared with egg, and shook his head. 'Not that it's likely one of them did it. No, I think we can rule them out.'

Jenny sighed. She'd rather feared as much.

'Sir George, Lady Vee, the colonel and Mrs Attling were all together at the time of the murder,' she murmured, missing the strange look Bishop sent her way. Then he was smearing tomato over his fried bread and crunching down in bliss. 'So that leaves us….' she finished softly.

Bishop nodded, looking at her closely. The fact that she had even dared to suspect Lord Avonsleigh and company had raised her inestimably in his opinion. Perhaps this wasn't going to be so bad after all.

At least the woman seemed to have some ability. 'Yes,' he agreed bluntly. 'And of you lot, Meecham and Gayle alibi each other. Lady Roberta and her art tutor do likewise. You and Elsie were together apart from that one time. By the way, I've had Myers do a dry run on that cellar thing, and Elsie *could* have done it, but only at a real stretch. And that's assuming that she knew that Ava Simmons was in the conservatory beforehand and that she caught her totally by surprise. Even so, she would have had to run at a fair old clip all the times in between. And I doubt the old girl has it in her.'

Jenny, remembering Elsie's silent gait and surprising agility, wasn't so sure. But she was not about to tell the inspector that.

'I don't see how Elsie could have known that Ava would be in the conservatory,' she said instead. 'Unless they'd arranged to meet there. You didn't find any note, did you?' she asked, without much hope.

Bishop shook his head, dunking his bacon in egg yolk. 'Nope. Only correspondence we found in her room was the odd letter to her father, and a letter from the Lady Beade Girls' School, offering Ava Simmons the post of fine art tutor. So we know she was leaving. Or seriously thinking about it, anyway.'

Jenny felt a cold shiver pass over her arms. She

couldn't help but frown, and the inspector paused in his ravenous eating, watching her closely. Catching his eye, Jenny gave a slight shrug. 'I find that very odd, Inspector. Ava had only been here a short time. Why would she seek a new job so soon?'

'Perhaps she knew what was coming. She'd made an enemy of someone here at the castle and thought she'd better get away. Quick. But just didn't make it in time.'

Jenny waved her hand. 'That's the first thing that occurred to me. But that's not what I meant. I've heard of the Lady Beade School. It's a top-notch affair. I can't understand why they'd offer a provincial gallery-owner's daughter the job of art tutor. I mean, they could have their pick. Now if it had been Malcolm Powell-Brooks they'd asked, I'd have understood it. He graduated from the Ruskin School of Fine Art in Oxford. But Ava Simmons?'

'She was the governess, or tutor, or whatever, to a lord's granddaughter,' Bishop pointed out, lamely.

'The Lady Beade has daughters of nobility coming out of their ears, Inspector,' Jenny pointed out with a small smile.

'No. It all strikes me as particularly odd. Do you think you could spare someone to go down to Lady Beade's and learn a little more? When did she apply? Before or after coming here? Why was she chosen? That sort of thing?'

Bishop nodded his head. He told himself it was the least he could do for someone who'd given him such a good breakfast. And he'd be humouring her ladyship, and her orders to keep the cook 'appraised'.

But in his heart, he suspected that Jenny Starling had *got* something. That she'd picked up on something that he had missed. Perhaps bringing the cook in on the investigation wouldn't be such a bad idea, after all.

BY NINE O'CLOCK the kitchen was full, and Bishop wisely absented himself. Jenny noted that most of her colleagues had regained their appetites. Only Meecham seemed uninterested in the feast, and nibbled desultorily on a piece of toast.

'Well, I suppose I'd better go up and see their nibs,' Malcolm said, a little nervously. 'I mean, someone has to take over Roberta's other lessons until a replacement has been found.'

'I'm sure they'll be relieved by your offer to stand in, Malcolm,' Gayle reassured him kindly, and watched him go with fond eyes.

Jenny glanced at her thoughtfully, then at the disappearing back of the art tutor, his white canvas smock showing up in the gloomier recess of the kitchen as he made his way to the door. So that's the way the wind blew, was it, Jenny mused? And worried. Would someone of Malcolm's ilk look on a maid-cum-tour-guide as a possible partner? She rather doubted it.

She shook her head, and hoped for the best. Gayle was a sensible girl. Let's just hope she was only being her usual, helpful self. Gayle as the peace-maker—not Gayle the smitten.

'I hear the police have been in the village, questioning people,' Janice said quietly, looking wan and dark-eyed.

'I expect they're learning all sorts of things by now.' She fingered a small brooch on her dark blue blouse nervously. Jenny had never seen her wearing it before. It was a silver ballerina, and looked totally out of place on her uniform.

Janice, unaware that she was fingering the brooch so compulsively, was thinking about her Danny. He'd been in just a little bit of bother with the police once. Something about not being properly insured on his motorbike. If word got back to her dad she'd be for it.

'Damn coppers,' Elsie barked. 'They hadn't better go near my old mum. Upsetting her and all.'

Jenny was surprised to hear that Elsie's mother still lived. She'd assumed that Elsie lived in at the castle, but perhaps she went home every night.

'Don't worry. All that's old news, Elsie dear. Why would the police want to know about it?' Gayle said, making the cook's ears perk up.

'What old news?' she asked, with a carefully general smile. Gayle, however, looked promptly disconcerted. She darted an apologetic glance to Elsie, who was showing definite signs of unease.

'Oh, nothing. Nothing really,' Gayle murmured lamely.

Jenny let the embarrassed silence deliberately drag. She glanced at Elsie who was staring into her cup of tea, then at Janice, who looked away quickly.

'Oh, well, I don't suppose it matters now,' Elsie finally said gruffly, the silence stretching her nerves. 'Me old mum never married me dad. Whoever he was,' Elsie added bitterly, lifting her chin defiantly.

Jenny met her gaze without expression. Although

illegitimacy meant nothing nowadays, she supposed that when Elsie was born, her mother would have been branded a scarlet woman. And even nowadays, in villages full of mostly older folk, she supposed something of a slur still attached itself to unmarried mothers.

'No, Elsie, I shouldn't think it matters a bit,' Jenny said kindly. 'You want some more kidneys? I fried some extra.'

For a second, the old kitchen maid's eyes swam, and Jenny realized, with a pang, that she'd been expecting some kind of cruel put down. Being born illegitimate had obviously been a burden that had haunted her all her life. It was all such a shame since nobody would give it a second thought nowadays.

Elsie, in fact, lived in unnecessary dread of the fact that their nibs might find out about it, and give her the sack. Even the old cook had always been a little scornful about it. That this new cook was so obviously different caught her off guard. She felt her stomach tremble in the way that it always did when she felt herself getting mushy, and she sniffed. Loudly.

'All right. Wouldn't say no,' she agreed, more harshly than she'd meant. It came out sounding deeply ungrateful. Jenny, however, didn't seem to notice. She returned with the frying pan and heaped out some kidneys onto Elsie's plate.

Elsie began to eat with evident pleasure.

But at the back of her eyes lurked a look of fear that pained Jenny for the rest of the day.

MALCOLM POWELL-BROOKS hesitated at the door to the breakfast-room. His palms felt just slightly damp. Then he knocked briskly, and tensed. He hated dealing directly with Lady Vee. She was just so damned formidable.

Her ladyship boomed at him to come in, and he obeyed, noting with relief that they had finished eating. Roberta glanced up and began to glow at the unexpected treat of seeing him so soon.

Lord Avonsleigh glanced at his granddaughter's shining eyes, and felt his lips twitch.

'Er, good morning, my lord, my lady,' he turned to each in turn, glanced at Roberta, wasn't quite sure what to say to her, and turned back to his lordship. He cleared his throat, opened his mouth, and wondered where to begin.

George smiled and rose. 'Sit down, dear fellow. What can we do for you?'

Lady Vee watched the art tutor seat himself and wished she was twenty years younger. She'd liked to flirt when she was a girl, and Mr Powell-Brooks was just the kind she went for. She couldn't blame Roberta for mooning over him like a lovesick calf. It was good for a girl to do so.

'I was wondering, that is, I thought I should come and offer my services as a temporary tutor that is, until, well, someone is sent to replace Miss Simmons. I have a fairly good working knowledge of literature,' Malcolm plunged on, feeling his palms growing wetter by the minute. 'I don't know much about…well, er, female deportment and that sort of thing, but I know a good bit about music, as you know, and philosophy and so on. Just until—'

'We get a replacement for poor Miss Simmons,' Lady

Vee interjected for him, noting his rising panic with a gentle smile. 'Quite so.' The dear boy was blushing to the roots of his hair.

'Yes, that's it,' Malcolm said gratefully.

'Thank you for the offer, Brooks,' Lord Avonsleigh said heartily. 'I think we'll have to take you up on it for the time being. Unless of course,' he added, winking across at his wife, 'Roberta objects?'

Lady Roberta most definitely didn't, and nearly fell over herself making it plain. Malcolm met his lordship's eye with an apologetic 'What can you do but wait until she grows out of it?' look, and relaxed.

He'd had to offer. It would have looked most odd if he hadn't.

'Well, I'm sure Lady Roberta can fill me in on Miss Simmons teaching regime. I….' He was getting to his feet, anxious to make his leave, when there was a tap on the door and Meecham walked in.

'Excuse me, my lord, but there's a gentleman here with an appointment to see Miss Simmons. I thought, under the circumstances….'

'Good grief, yes.' Lord Avonsleigh rose, and smiled as a tall, silver-haired man, who was eighty if he was a day, walked into the room. 'I think you'd better get Inspector Bishop, Meecham,' he said, walking forward and holding out his hand.

Before it was taken, however, Bishop appeared at the doorway. Nothing went on in this castle that he didn't know about, for he'd seconded a few constables from Bicester to patrol the place on the pretext of providing extra security. In reality, they were his eyes and ears, and badly needed they were too.

The bewildered old man glanced at the inspector, then at Avonsleigh, looking distinctly puzzled. If he'd known that Ava was going to have him meet his lordship he'd have worn his best tie. 'I'm sorry, Lord Avonsleigh. I'm afraid I don't quite understand.'

Vee went forward and gently led him to a seat. 'Tea, Meecham,' she said briskly. 'We've run into a spot of trouble, I'm afraid, Mr…?'

'Oh, excuse me. Grover, Anthony Grover. How do you do?'

She took his hand and pulled out a seat close to him. 'You've come to see Miss Simmons, you say?' she probed gently, not even glancing in Bishop's direction.

Unable to do a damned thing about it, Bishop took a seat and ground his teeth.

'Yes, that's right,' Anthony Grover said, looking around, his watery blue eyes falling on a Turner landscape and lighting up before returning to those of Lady Vee. 'Is there something wrong?' His old voice wavered, as if it was all getting to be just a little too much. Vee brightened in relief as Meecham returned with the tea. The poor old boy was going to need it.

'I think you'd better have three sugars, Mr Grover,' she said, gently hinting at shocks to come. 'Did you know Miss Simmons well?'

Meecham retired. Malcolm Powell-Brooks, who'd sunk back into his seat and was wishing himself miles away, held his breath.

'Oh, yes, since she was a girl, really. I knew her father slightly.' His lips twisted into a distasteful grimace.

'Oh dear,' Lady Vee said on a huge sigh. 'I'm afraid I have bad news. There's not a kind way of doing this, I'm afraid, but, well, Miss Simmons was killed yesterday. Murdered, I'm very sorry to say.'

Anthony Grover went grey, and his rheumatic hands clenched his cup so hard that the fine china looked in imminent danger of breaking. 'Murdered? How? Who?' he spluttered, his voice turning into a croak.

'We don't know, I'm afraid,' she said, reaching out and holding the old man's hand. It was deathly cold.

'Oh, poor little Ava,' Anthony said. 'When she wrote and asked me to come and see her, I thought it was—'

'She wrote to you?' Bishop asked, unable to restrain himself any longer.

Startled by the abrupt question and loud, unsympathetic voice, Anthony Grover half-turned to meet the policeman's alert gaze, the tea sloshing dangerously in his cup. 'Yes. I received the letter two days ago. She asked me to come and see her today at ten o'clock.'

'Did she say why she wanted to see you?' Bishop asked, then, as an afterthought, introduced himself.

'No. She said she wanted my opinion on something. She was always coming to me for advice. She looked on me like an uncle, I think. Her father, well, her father was always busy with the gallery. He had little time for her.'

He doesn't like Ava Simmons's father, Bishop thought instantly. He'd have to have Mr Simmons senior checked out rather more thoroughly. 'I see. And she said nothing else in this letter?' he prompted.

'No, Inspector. Nothing.'

'Was the tone of the letter unusual in any way? Did she sound worried or frightened?'

'No, not that I could tell. I thought she might want my advice on text books. I was a teacher you know. Art.'

'I see,' Bishop said, disappointed. Another dead end. He couldn't even stretch a point and wonder if Anthony Grover were the missing boyfriend. Women might go for older men, but not that much older.

He heard a quiet sigh and glanced across, surprised to see Malcolm Powell-Brooks cowering in his chair.

'When was the last time you saw Miss Simmons?' Bishop pressed on. He had no clues, no leads, and was determined to milk any evidence at all for all it was worth.

'Oh, months ago,' Anthony Grover said, his eyes watering. 'I never thought it would be the last time.'

'No, of course not,' Vee said kindly, patting the old man's hand and giving Bishop a killing look. 'Drink some tea, Mr Grover. It will make you feel better.'

Anthony Grover drank some tea. Avonsleigh caught Bishop's eye and beckoned him over into one corner to grill him on his progress. Malcolm took the opportunity to leave, Roberta quickly trailing after him.

Vee took Anthony's arm. What he needed was distracting. 'I daresay you'd like to see some of our paintings, Mr Grover?'

The old man perked up a little. 'Well, yes, I would. Avonsleigh has such a wonderful reputation in the art world, as you know. I quite envy the experts you allow to come and look around. I daresay you choose them carefully? Everyone must press you for an invitation.'

'Oh, yes, well, one must do one's best,' she said airily. 'And our resident art expert lets us know when the paintings need cleaning. Wouldn't do to have them dirty, eh?'

The old man looked at her, hiding his smile. She was a charming, warm, eccentric character but was an obvious Philistine when it came to art. 'There was just that Turner that caught my eye,' Anthony murmured, steering her in its direction. And Lady Vee, glad to have taken his mind off the tragedy, smiled and let him have full rein.

As Bishop filled in Lord Avonsleigh on his progress so far—which was frankly none—Anthony Grover stared in astonishment at the Avonsleigh Turner.

He stared at it for quite some time.

NINE

JENNY STOOD ASIDE to let Meecham and his elderly companion pass by in the small corridor. She watched them go for a moment, a worried frown on her face. The old man had looked decidedly shaken. She hoped it was nothing serious.

Glad that she had taken the time before going to bed last night to do a thorough tour of the castle, and at last get all the rooms and their layout (more or less) straight in her mind, she had found the breakfast-room with little trouble. Now she knocked on the door, waited for Lady Vee to boom her usual welcome and walked in.

Vee glanced up, a smile immediately lighting up her face and setting her jowls quivering. 'Miss Starling, how wonderful. Any news?'

Jenny smiled, taking the seat indicated. 'I'm sorry, no. The police don't seem to be much further forward. Inspector Bishop told me the findings of the pathology report. It was Ava's blood on the dagger, of course, and the wound was fairly consistent with the murder weapon being the dagger. So, no surprises there. Though there is one interesting little thing I picked up on.'

She went on to explain about the curious letter from the Lady Beade School, her ladyship agreeing with her that it was most odd.

'I for one don't believe she meant to leave us,' Avon-sleigh, sitting by the fire with a newspaper in his lap, spoke up for the first time.

Jenny glanced at him with renewed respect. 'I agree, my lord. Although I only knew her for barely a day, she didn't strike me as a woman getting ready to leave here. In fact, she seemed, if anything, determined to protect Lady Roberta,' she added quietly, wondering what re-action the bait would get.

Vee laughed. 'Oh she was, bless her heart. Why, she came to us only a week ago and told us that Ro-berta was forming an "undesirable attachment" to Mr Powell-Brooks,' she confirmed, her eyes twinkling. 'Of course, we already knew that—we've got eyes in our heads, haven't we? We told her that Roberta, for all her exuberance, was actually a very steady and re-liable sort of girl. She might moon over our handsome Mr Powell-Brooks, but then, what teenage girl wouldn't moon over him?' Her eyebrow rose in a question, and Jenny smiled back her answer. 'But she's far too sen-sible to dream it would come to anything more than a bit of mutual mild flirting.'

'And how did Ava react to that?' Jenny asked curi-ously.

'She seemed a little taken aback that we knew,' Lady Vee replied after some thought. 'I got the impression that she believed we lived in an ivory tower and didn't know the more mundane details of what went on in our little fiefdom. It was really kind of her to worry, and we told her so, but when we explained that we'd already had a quiet little word with Malcolm about it, she seemed satisfied.'

'Really?' This time it was Jenny's eyebrow that rose. Vee settled herself back. It had been a long time since she'd had a good gossip with someone worthy of it.

'Yes. You see, Roberta was making calf-eyes at him only a matter of days after his arrival. That would have been over a year ago now, when she was only fifteen. Well, we weren't really worried, of course, but thought it best to have word with him. Just in case he had some silly idea about marrying into money, and all that.'

'Oh quite,' Jenny said hastily.

'We want none of that,' her ladyship said with a small shiver. 'But, as it happened, we needn't have worried. Mr Powell-Brooks was very good about it. Rather a quiet type, for all his good looks. He had to splutter about a bit since he's not particularly erudite, but for all that he made it plain that what he wanted was a nice steady job and nothing more. He explained that it was the privilege of living at Avonsleigh, surrounded by all this....'—Vee waved a casual hand at the wall, on which reposed Gainsboroughs, Constables and Turners, as if they were printed posters—'that made him want to work here. In fact, he was far more anxious about Roberta's little infatuation than we were—in case we gave him the sack, you see?'

Avonsleigh rustled his paper, and both women turned to look at him. 'Thing is, the fellow confided in me that a spell here would set him up for life. In the art world, that is. He hopes to go on to something in a museum apparently. And having the name Avonsleigh on his résumé would be the lynchpin. Poor chap was dead scared Roberta's crush would put the kibosh on it.'

'In the end,' Vee picked up the tale, '*we* ended up reassuring *him*!'

Jenny nodded. 'I see. He's of a much more practical turn of mind than you might think to look at him.'

'Yes,' her ladyship agreed. 'And the more we've come to know him, the more relaxed we've become. He humours Roberta without encouraging her, you see. That way, her grand passion can gradually fizzle out without her feelings being hurt.'

Jenny, remembering their light bantering, nodded. 'So he knows which side his bread is buttered?'

'Exactly.' Her twinkling eyes suddenly glittered into a hardening expression. 'We could make life very hard for our Mr Powell-Brooks if we'd a mind to, and he knows it.'

Jenny nodded. 'So Miss Simmons never mentioned it again?' she prompted, remembering the way Ava had looked upon her charge and the art tutor so disapprovingly the day Jenny had first arrived at the castle.

'No. Mind you, Roberta got to hear about Miss Simmons telling tales. The walls have ears in this place.' Her ladyship sighed. 'Little minx knows how to throw a temper tantrum when she wants to, let me tell you! She accused her governess of spying on her and telling lies, and trying to ruin her life. The usual dramatics. She demanded we fire her immediately. We told her in no uncertain terms that wasn't on, and that it was part of a governess's job to keep an eagle eye out for her charge's welfare.'

'Hmm,' Jenny said. So that was why Roberta hadn't liked her governess. Hardly surprising! The question was—how far did that acrimony really go? She had a feeling that it was not all that far. But what if the girl had really fancied herself in love with her art tutor? Teenagers were notoriously unpredictable, what with all those hormones raging about. But could she really see Roberta killing her governess in thwarted rage? It was an uncomfortable thought.

'Did Mr Powell-Brooks know about Ava's disapproval of him?' she asked delicately.

Lady Vee glanced up at her sharply, aware of the direction of her thoughts, and felt her respect for this Amazon of a cook swell even further. 'I would think he must have done. Roberta's not the sort to keep secrets. When she's upset, the whole world has to know about it—and why.'

Jenny sighed. But if Malcolm knew his job was safe, he had no real reason to kill Ava, had he? Besides, he and Roberta were together the whole afternoon. Unless they were in it together, maybe? No, now she was being fanciful. Besides, Jenny was sure that Roberta's reaction on hearing the news of Ava's death was perfectly genuine.

So, another dead end there.

She sighed deeply. 'The thing is, there seems to be no reason for it at all,' she said at last, feeling vexed. 'I shall have to go to the village and ask around. Try to get some kind of a feel for what's been going on up here.' She suddenly realized that might sound insulting and looked up quickly, but Lady Vee was already nodding her head.

'Good idea. Between you and me, I don't think this Inspector Bishop chap has much go in him. George had a word with him this morning, when Ava's friend showed up, and he hadn't got anywhere, had he, George?'

Avonsleigh, buried deep in the cricket scores, grunted.

'Ava's friend?' Jenny prompted, and Lady Vee obligingly gave her an accurate account of the old man's arrival and the subsequent revelations. Jenny listened and wondered. Ava Simmons had definitely been up to something. Something that had resulted in her murder. But what?

'I understand it's all being kept out of the papers,' Jenny mused.

'As far as one can. But one can't control the gossip in the village though. Or expect one's friends to…oh hell's bells, that reminds me. Miss Starling, we're giving a dinner party tomorrow night. It was arranged weeks ago, and I quite forgot about it.'

'I expect people will know it's been cancelled, m'dear,' his lordship said, and then froze as two pairs of disbelieving female eyes shot his way.

'Don't be so daft, George,' Vee said in total disregard for her husband's noble dignity. 'Everyone will be absolutely gasping to come. I bet they can't wait to set foot in the place. I shall probably end up giving them a guided tour of the conservatory and everything.'

Jenny nodded sagely. 'People are such ghouls.'

'Quite, besides, if we cancelled….' she broke off and

glanced guiltily at her husband, then she met the cook's eye, and nodded grimly.

Jenny understood exactly what was on Vee's mind. If they cancelled, people might start to think in very peculiar ways. Lord Avonsleigh was late middle-aged, and Ava had been a reasonably attractive younger woman. And soon the rumour that there was no smoke without fire would take hold, and who knew where that would end? No, it was best to carry on as normal.

Again the two women nodded at each, in complete understanding. He must be protected at all costs.

'How many are coming, my lady?' she asked, and Vee frowned.

'I suppose we'd better get it sorted out now. Let's see, there'll be eight altogether. Old Stebbins can't touch fat, and Ethel doesn't like anything green, and Jasper Cotton is a total hypochondriac. See to it, will you, Miss Starling?' she asked, and everyone in the room knew that it was seen to.

Just then Meecham entered. 'The vicar and his wife, my lady.'

Behind him came a dog-collared individual, so small and pucker-faced that he instantly reminded Jenny of a pug. 'Lady Vee, I thought we simply had to come....' he began, oozing concern.

And so it begins, Jenny thought sadly, and took the opportunity to excuse herself. She had a menu to prepare. And a trip to the village was definitely in order.

First, however, she went to the kitchen and removed the coffee and walnut cake from the larder. She'd cooked it first thing, and it was just nicely cooled. She quickly transferred it to a silver platter, put the domed lid on top to keep any flies out, and left it on the sideboard.

A moment later, Meecham returned, carrying a pile of silver, which he dumped onto the sideboard with a small sigh.

'Work's by far the best thing, Mr Meecham,' Jenny said gently. 'Keeps your mind off things.'

The butler nodded and went to his pantry to get his cleaning things. After the incident with the dagger, he didn't think he could clean anything unless it was out here in the open, with everybody watching him.

Janice came in for the tea things Jenny had automatically prepared, knowing her ladyship would have ordered it for her—albeit unwanted—guests. Meecham saw Janice lift the tea tray from the sideboard, and quickly took control of it. 'You know I always serve when there are guests, Janice,' he chided.

'There's cake on the platter,' Jenny said, already on her way out.

Meecham retrieved the domed dish, frowned at the weight and hoped Miss Starling didn't have an unexpectedly heavy hand with cakes, and returned to the breakfast-room.

Over on the sofa, Lady Vee was fending off the vicar's wife whilst agreeing how terrible it all was. Avonsleigh, obliged to give up his favourite chair, was now sitting by the table. Meecham put the tea things onto the small coffee table in front of Lady Vee and retired to the main table to cut the cake.

He carefully put out the gold and navy-blue Worcester plates and eighteenth-century silver cake forks and lifted the silver dome. And there, blinking up at him, was Henry. The tortoise opened its mouth as if about to ask the butler what he thought he was playing at, and without blinking an eye, Meecham quickly and neatly covered the reptile again with the domed lid and cast a hasty glance around. Her ladyship was still entertaining the vicar's wife, and the vicar himself was still in his lordship's usurped seat, roasting his toes in the hearth. Meecham glanced to his right, where Lord Avonsleigh was barely inches away, eyes twinkling. 'The cook seems to have left the cherry off the top of the cake, my lord,' he murmured. 'I think perhaps I should retrieve it.'

Avonsleigh nodded solemnly. 'I think you better had, Meecham,' he agreed, and wandered over to the fire to chat to the vicar about Sri Lanka's chances in the next test match.

Meecham sprinted back to the kitchen, resisting the urge to drop-kick the tortoise out of the back door. On the sideboard was another domed platter, and this he lifted, spying a splendidly iced and nut-decorated cake underneath. He then sprinted back to the breakfast-room, caught his breath, entered and proceeded to serve the cake with perfect aplomb.

THE VILLAGE OF Upper Caulcott was typical of north Oxfordshire, except that it had managed to keep a small post office-cum-general shop with a small butcher's department. There Jenny made the proprietor's day by ordering prime venison, two brace of pheasant and eight medium-sized freshly caught trout, to be delivered to the castle as and when possible.

Mr Jenkins promised delivery soon, and watched the new cook go towards the post office counter, wishing he'd had the gall to ask her about the murder. The wife would kill him when she heard about the visit but that he had no titbits of gossip to tell her. The whole village was positively buzzing. The trouble was, the new cook up at the castle was both beautiful and large, a combination which had always kept him tongue-tied.

The lady behind the counter quickly sold her some stamps, and was able to give her directions to the house of Elsie's mother.

Jenny was not surprised to see that Miss Bingham lived in the poorest-looking cottage in the village, a two-up, two-down affair of badly rotted casements and paint-flaked doors. She knocked briskly at the front door and waited. A sound from around the back had her opening a rusty side gate and taking the garden path past rows of neatly cultivated vegetables.

An old woman stood at the end of the garden, tying up runner beans. She had Elsie's scowl and stooped, overworked stance. Jenny wondered how much the old lady relied on her daughter's wages, and had a fair idea that she didn't grow so many vegetables simply as a hobby, and vowed to send Elsie home with something nourishing in a pot every day from now on.

She saw the old lady notice her and stiffen. 'What do you want then?' she challenged gruffly.

Jenny smiled and approached her, careful not to bruise any of the cabbages growing right up against a narrow grass path. 'I'm the new cook up at the castle,' she began, and saw the old woman pale in fright. 'I just wanted to stop by and say hello, and tell you what a wonderful helper your daughter is, and what a good job she's doing,' she added hastily.

Miss Bingham relaxed. 'Ah, Elsie's a good worker. Always was. Want a cup of tea?'

Jenny accepted, knowing it would have been a gross insult to refuse. She followed the old woman into the dark, sparsely furnished cottage. The tiny kitchen boasted two hard-backed chairs and Jenny took one, watching the old woman as she set about making the tea. 'Take milk?' the old lady asked abruptly.

'Yes, please.'

'I suppose their nibs are glad to have another cook at last,' Miss Bingham finally said, taking the other chair, which wobbled alarmingly. Looking down, Jenny could see where two of its legs had been crudely mended.

'Yes, they are,' she responded mildly. 'I must say though, it's been rather awkward, starting a new job only to have something so awful happen.'

The old woman's hands closed around her mug in a compulsive movement that made Jenny's eyes widen.

'I dare say,' she muttered, something so neutral in her voice that it had almost the opposite effect of making it sound furtive.

'The police, of course, are being such a nuisance, questioning everyone,' Jenny carried on carefully. She had an idea that once Miss Bingham clammed up, there'd be no prising the old lady's lips apart again. So she mustn't scare her. 'They do keep on and on about things.' She sighed heavily.

'Well, we ain't got nothing to worry about—Elsie and me, we're all right,' the old woman said firmly. And couldn't have made it more obvious that she was almost sick with fright.

'I know a little bit about the way the police work,' Jenny said, then seeing the old woman's eyes sharpen in alarm, added quickly, 'We had a robbery once at a restaurant where I worked. They just poke and pry and dig into everyone's backgrounds and learn things that don't have a thing to do with the crime in question,' she continued craftily. 'I was so embarrassed I had to leave. Still, to be fair, I don't suppose they can know what's important and what isn't, so they have to check out every little thing. Trouble is, all us innocent ones suffer too, just so they can get to the guilty.'

Miss Bingham paled even further, but said nothing. Jenny took a sip of tea, desperately trying to think of a way to move things forward.

'I dare say that's so,' Miss Bingham said heavily at last, and then glanced up at the cook, her eyes small and dark, and reminding Jenny of those of a chicken. A chicken with a sharp beak—a chicken that would do anything, and tackle anyone, who threatened her chick. 'You say you like my Elsie?'

'Yes, I do, I admire her very much,' Jenny said, honestly. 'She's a hard worker, which is rare these days, and I think she's probably had a hard life. She confided in me about, well, how things haven't been easy for you either.'

'She did, did she?' the old woman said, obviously surprised. 'Well, I suppose it was bound to come out. There's folks in this village old enough to remember….'

'Remember what?' she asked gently, holding her breath as the old woman seemed to hesitate.

'Hmm? Oh, to remember who it was who got me into trouble all them years ago. He were a local lad, should have married me, but he didn't. He weren't already married or nothing like that, and his dad was a farm worker, just like mine. But he had big ideas, did Basil. Even then. And I suppose you have to give the devil his due, he made all his big ideas come true.'

The old woman sighed. 'But it was terrible har Me dad threw me out when he heard I was in the far ily way, and I had to have our Elsie in one of the women's shelters. Then his lordship, the old lord would be, he let me have this cottage for a peppe rent. I used to work at Miltons, the factory in Bic Worked there for years I did, till it closed down. made enough to keep us both going. Then Elsie l school and they took her on as a kitchen maid up at t castle, and she's been there ever since. But all this tim Basil was living it up in leaps and bounds. Did real well for himself without a wife and kiddie tying hi down,' she added bitterly. 'But the thing is….' The ol woman suddenly reached across and grabbed Jenny' hand in a fierce grip, her eyes wide with fear and beg ging for understanding.

'Elsie took it all so very hard. She found out whe she was working up at the castle who her dad was. never talked about him, see. She was about twenty whe she found out. I talked her out of going to see him—I knew he was a selfish sod, and wouldn't want to know about a grown up daughter—especially one who was nothing more than skivvy. I told her it would do no good. Basil was always a hard man, even when he was a young 'un. Oh he was a charmer all right, I wasn't the only girl he managed to sweet talk into giving him what he wanted. But, as he got older, I reckon he got meaner. You could ask Mr Meecham and his daughter about that,' she added, making Jenny blink in surprise.

Then the old woman shook her head. 'But there, that's not for me to talk about. I got troubles of my own,' she said, dampening Jenny's hopes of getting yet more information from her. 'If them coppers find out who Elsie's dad is, well, they might get the wrong end of the stick, mightn't they? Then what'll we do?' she wailed, suddenly looking very old and frightened indeed. Instinctively, Jenny tightened her own grip on the old woman's hand comfortingly.

But she needed to get things clarified. She hadn't wanted to interrupt Miss Bingham when she was speaking, but now she had no choice.

'But why should they get the wrong end of the stick, Miss Bingham?' she asked gently. 'What has Basil to do with the murder up at the castle?'

Miss Bingham stared at her as if she was stupid. 'Because Basil was *her* dad too.'

And then, suddenly, Jenny understood. She felt a cold, nasty feeling in her stomach and swallowed hard. 'You mean, Basil was…?'

'Basil Simmons,' Miss Bingham said heavily and nodded.

'Him that owns that fancy art gallery.'

And Jenny could now see the old woman's predicament. Ava Simmons's father was also Elsie's father. They were sisters—well, half-sisters to be precise.

And Elsie must have known it.

But had said nothing. Because Jenny was sure, looking back on her brief time spent with Ava when she was alive, that the governess had had no inkling that Elsie was of her own flesh and blood.

TEN

Jenny began to puff as she climbed the hill. Above her, the castle towered and glowered, blocking out the light and casting her in its shadow.

Miss Bingham's words were still ringing in her ears. According to the old lady, the fact that 'that girl who got herself killed' was Elsie's sister, didn't mean 'my Elsie had gone and done it'.

No, it didn't, she mused. But it certainly gave her a motive, Jenny thought, pausing by the side of the road to catch her breath. Here, she took the opportunity to look around her. Spread out below her was Upper Caulcott. Beyond the village a winding river cut through meadows of wild flowers, planted barley, and grazing black-and-white cattle. Willows lined the river, and birds flitted and dashed, busy raising chicks. It all looked so beautifully pastoral, and the castle itself, so utterly British.

And yet something, somewhere, was utterly rotten.

Jenny sighed wearily and continued her climb, for the first time feeling reluctant to go back to the castle. The perfect job of less than three days ago was already becoming a burden on her shoulders.

But it could all come right again—or so she hoped— with her usual optimism. Once this murder was solved, the castle would soon recover its warm, friendly atmosphere. Life would gentle itself down. The years would pass, and she could settle like sediment in the first, truly permanent job of her career. It was probably time for her to settle down. But first things first. She sighed, and forced her mind back to the matters in hand.

So Elsie had always known that Ava Simmons was her half-sister. But Basil Simmons had married Ava's mother, whereas he'd rejected her own. Ava had had a fine education, and had become tutor to a Lord's granddaughter. She looked, spoke, and acted like a lady of some standing. Ava got to call the kitchen maid Elsie.

Elsie, on the other hand, had been labelled a bastard all her life. She'd have been taunted by the children at the local primary school, and ostracized by their parents. She'd have left school and gone straight into the most menial work available. Elsie was old before her time. She had had to work like a horse, forced to call her own sister Miss Simmons. And a thing like that could eat at the soul. The injustices of life had been known to drive people to the brink of madness. How Elsie must have resented the new governess! Seeing every day in Ava Simmons what she herself had missed in life. What she herself could have been, had Basil Simmons married her own mother. People would have called *her* Miss Simmons. Instead she had to scrub the kitchen floor. Wait on everyone. Fill the slot of the lowliest maid in the castle. How could she stand it? And had she finally, in a burst of resentment and hatred, killed her own sister?

Jenny hoped not. Jenny very *fervently* hoped not. But one thing was for sure: Inspector Bishop would just have to find out about Elsie's parentage for himself. Until she had some genuine proof of guilt, she was not about to go and add to her kitchen-maid's misery.

WHEN JENNY RETURNED to the kitchen, Malcolm Powell-Brooks was washing out some little glass jars in the sink. Janice, Meecham and Gayle were all sitting down to their tea break and finishing off the walnut and coffee cake. No doubt the vicar and his lady wife had left, their curiosity finally satisfied.

'I hope those are not oils, or anything poisonous, Mr Powell-Brooks,' Jenny said sharply, watching bright azure-stained water slide down the drain. 'I do have to prepare food here, remember.'

'Oh no, nothing like that,' Malcolm assured her, rinsing out a mint-green stained jar and standing it on the sideboard. 'It's watercolour. See how easily it washes out? A good spurt from the tap,'—he demonstrated on a jar of sickly yellow—'and it's gone.' He presented the clean glass jar for her inspection.

Jenny nodded dubiously. She didn't approve of strange goings-on at her sink. She poured herself a cup of tea out and sat down opposite Janice, who glanced at the art tutor's back and grinned.

Leaning closer to the cook, she lowered her voice. 'Don't you believe it, Miss Starling. He washes out oils too. I saw him only last week cleaning out a jar so thoroughly he used an old knife to delve down around the bottom of the inside rim. He even used some bleach, and was cleaning it for a good ten minutes. No way *that* could have been watercolour.'

Jenny sighed. 'Well, whatever the old cook let him get away with, he won't get away with it now,' she said firmly, and resolved to keep a careful eye on the art tutor in future.

Elsie chose that moment to come up from one of the cellars. She was carrying a huge sack of potatoes. 'You said you was doing shepherd's pie,' she said, dumping them over by the sink, unceremoniously shoving the art tutor to one side. Her bulk and surliness meant Malcolm didn't even sigh in protest. 'Their nibs likes their pie with lots of spuds,' Elsie added, grabbing a cup and sitting down heavily.

Jenny, with her new knowledge, looked at her sharply, and what she saw gave her cause to think. Elsie's eyes were red-rimmed and slightly swollen, so she'd obviously been crying. Crying for her dead sister perhaps? It had probably only just now hit her—she had lost a sister, and it wouldn't matter that that sister had not even known that she, Elsie, had existed. Losing a relative, no matter what the circumstances, was bound to tell on you sooner or later.

Jenny was glad to see the tears. But they proved nothing.

'Well, I'd better take these back to the minx,' Malcolm said, picking up the clean little jars and putting them in one of his painting smock's many pockets. 'Janice, did you get me that red paint that I asked you for on—' he broke off as he realized that it had been the day of the murder. 'Oh, forget it. I'll get some more myself. I have to go into Bicester later on.'

Janice watched him go, biting her lip and fingering

her ridiculous brooch. Then she too jumped up, muttering something about dusting, and gave the brooch a final tweak. Jenny wished she would stop it. It was getting on her nerves.

When the door had closed behind her, Elsie too made a move. 'I'd better go see old Seth. You want some tomatoes out of the hothouse?' she asked.

Jenny did. Tomatoes did wonders to pep up minced beef. The cook watched her go then turned to look at Meecham. 'I went to see Miss Bingham this morning,' she said quietly. 'I think she's worried about Elsie.'

Meecham cut himself another slice of the delicious cake and wondered where Henry was. He worried when he couldn't keep an eye on that reptile. One more incident like this morning's and his heart wouldn't stand it. Thank goodness only his lordship had noticed his blunder.

'Oh?' he murmured, vaguely aware that the cook was waiting for a response. 'I don't think she need worry.' Suddenly he stopped slicing and looked across at the cook. He paled slightly. 'You mean, does she think there might be another murder? That one of us might be killed?'

Jenny quickly shook her head. 'Oh no. Not that. No, I don't think there's a madman on the loose in the castle or anything. I think she was more worried that the police might get it in into their heads to arrest Elsie.'

'But that's silly,' Gayle chimed in with a small, nervous laugh. 'Why should they do that? Elsie had no reason to kill Miss Simmons.' She reached for the sugar bowl and spooned in a level teaspoon, her hands shaking slightly.

So they know who her father is, Jenny thought accurately. They'd always known.

'No, perhaps not. But she seemed to think someone else at the castle might have reason to, well…disapprove of Miss Simmons,' she continued, watching them both carefully.

She had not forgotten Miss Bingham's quickly cut-off hint that the Meechams themselves might have a skeleton of their own in their closet that they'd be anxious to keep concealed.

Meecham swallowed and glanced across at his daughter. Gayle was staring at the cook with a level, assessing glance that made Jenny want to shift uncomfortably in her seat. She did no such thing, of course, but gazed back, equally coolly.

'You *have* been busy, haven't you, Miss Starling?' Gayle said finally. But there was no malice in her voice; just the hard, heavy ring of reality. 'I've been doing my homework too, as it happens. I thought the police were treating you a little differently from all the rest of us. And it couldn't only have been because you were so new here.'

'Gayle!' Meecham said, aghast.

'So I went into town myself this morning,' Gayle continued, ignoring her father's reproof, 'and went to the newspaper office. I asked around, made a phone call or two to a reporter friend of mine and, guess what? Your name rang a bell. In fact, it rang several bells.'

'Gayle, what are you saying?' Meecham asked, looking at the cook in some alarm.

Jenny took a sip of tea, and placidly let Gayle get on with it.

'It seems, Father, that Miss Starling is something of an amateur detective. In fact, you have three solved murders to your credit, don't you, Miss Starling?'

Jenny sighed and nodded. 'I have been able to help the police on the odd occasion,' she agreed modestly.

'And you're helping them now, aren't you?' Gayle continued, still in the same, flat monotone. 'I daresay Lady Vee wants some eyes and ears below stairs.'

'Now that's enough,' Meecham said. 'You won't speak about her ladyship in that way.'

Gayle reached across and patted her father's hand reassuringly. It was almost, Jenny thought, as if *she* were the parent, and Meecham the child. 'No, Father. But Miss Starling has been busy. You know about Elsie, don't you?'

Jenny nodded. There was no point in denying it.

'And you won't stop digging until you know everything about us, will you?' she added fatalistically.

'Gayle, I really don't think….' Meecham began nervously, but Gayle again patted his hand, effectively silencing him.

'It's better if it comes from us, Father,' Gayle said with a sigh. 'Besides, the police are bound to find out sooner or later. You see, Miss Starling, we weren't always tour guides, or even butler and maid. My father and mother once owned a farm. Oh, it was a small farm, and not very prosperous, but it was theirs. They owned the land, they farmed it, and were well respected by their peers. This was to the west of here. Near the Gloucestershire border. I lived on the farm until I was eight.'

Gayle paused to glance at her father, who was staring down at his uneaten cake, his face a picture of misery.

'We had a bad winter one year. Lost too many sheep. We had to take out a bank loan.'

Even when she was eight, Jenny thought astutely, it was 'we'. Not 'Mum and Dad', but 'we'. Gayle must have had to grow up very quickly, the cook thought, bracing herself for the tale of woe to come. And there must be one to come. Farmers and landowners didn't become servants by choice.

'For a while, it looked as if things would pick up. But then there was a second bad winter.' Gayle sighed, obviously remembering it all very well indeed. 'My mother was the daughter of a local factory owner. It wasn't a big factory, not a nationally known one or anything like that, but it had done all right in the past. Her father gave my mother a painting as a wedding present. Oh, it was not by Turner, or Constable, like they have around here, but one of the minor Victorians. It was a pretty picture of a girl with long blonde curly hair cuddling a red-setter dog. Very pretty. Very popular.'

Gayle picked up a spoon and began to stir her tea. 'We decided to sell it in order to pay off the bank and keep the farm. We took it to an art dealer we knew. He'd just opened a new shop in Bicester. We'd seen it written up in the newspapers.'

Jenny felt her spine tingle. 'This art dealer...?'

she prompted, her voice bland, but she already knew the answer.

Gayle nodded. 'Basil Simmons. He told us that the painting wasn't worth much. This was before the Victorians became so popular. He said nobody wanted 'chocolate box' pictures much. Said the painting wasn't even that well painted, and that it wasn't by a very well-known artist. But he said he'd buy it, if we were really desperate.'

'And of course, we were,' Meecham spoke for the first time, his voice bleak with remembrance.

'My mother managed to get the price up high enough to pay off the bank. Just. So we sold it, paid the bank, and returned to the farm.'

'But we didn't have enough money to buy more sheep to cover those we'd lost. Also, the cost of feed and grain had soared,' Meecham added, sounding for the first time like the farmer he had once been.

'You lost the farm,' Jenny said flatly, with some effort managing to keep her heartfelt pity out of her voice.

'Yes,' Meecham echoed sadly. 'We lost the farm. We moved to Banbury, into a poky little flat. I got a job in a hardware store. My wife had to take on any odd job she could find. Working part-time, for a pittance. By then, her own father had died and her brother had inherited the factory. He had seven children of his own; he couldn't help us. The heart just seemed to go right out of Judith,' Meecham said, his voice trembling as he remembered. 'Within a year we'd lost her.'

He glanced up as Gayle took his other hand and held on to it fiercely.

And so Gayle had taken her mother's place, Jenny thought shrewdly. At, what? Ten, eleven years old? Cooking, cleaning, and probably taking over the family finances.

'I finally took on a more permanent job as butler to one of the local families,' Meecham continued the story of his life. 'The old man who'd been the butler there for years and years, taught me all he knew about the job before he left, and I found I was good at it. Then, I came here, about, oh, eight years ago. And since then, we've been really happy, haven't we, Gayle?' he asked anxiously.

Gayle nodded quickly. 'Oh yes, Father. I love it here,' she assured him. 'I took over as her ladyship's maid when the old one left. Not many girls can say they are maids to a real lady these days,' she said, her voice deliberately excited. 'Princess Diana made all that seem so glam.'

But was she really happy here? Jenny wondered. Or was it all a sham, to help reassure her father that he was not a failure?

'Yes, but I still don't quite understand why Miss Bingham should think you might have a reason to come under suspicion,' Jenny said, putting it as delicately as she could.

Opposite her, Gayle's lips twisted. 'Oh, but she was right,' she said, her voice hardening. 'You see, about three years after we'd sold the painting to Mr Simmons, we were passing his shop and saw our painting in the window. It had a sold sticker on it, and the price was still on the frame. It was, well, let's just say it was for a whole lot more than he paid us for it. A whole lot more.'

Jenny could well imagine. She was beginning to build up a good, solid picture of Basil Simmons from various sources, and it was not pretty.

'When I tackled him about it,' Meecham said heavily, anger at last creeping into his voice, 'he said that he'd deliberately held it back until people had started wanting Victoriana again. He said it went in waves. That art was like clothes—things came into fashion and went out. He said that now people wanted pretty paintings. And that the painting had turned out to be by quite a well-known artist after all.'

Meecham swallowed, his face becoming pinched with resentment. 'I threatened to call in the police, but he just laughed. He said that I had agreed to sell it, and that was that. Said it was a case of seller beware.'

Meecham's hands clenched into fists, turning his knuckles white. Wordlessly, Gayle reached across and the two held hands tightly. 'I became really angry. I told him he couldn't get away with cheating people. I said that I had a good case for fraud. But he just laughed, and asked me if I could afford a lawyer, and to be tied up in the court system for months. Then he said that everyone would think me a fool for being taken in and would laugh behind my back. And what would my employer think about that? And he was right, of course, on all counts. I couldn't afford a court case, but he was doing well by then. His shop was making a lot of money. And no employer wants a butler who's in the public eye. By our very nature, we have to be discreet. We have to be unobtrusive.'

Jenny nodded. And Meecham liked being unobtrusive, this she understood instinctively. Life had dealt him some very hard knocks, and he didn't possess the kind of character to withstand them easily.

No wonder he clung on possessively to his life here in the castle. His lordship was a good and kind employer. His life was ordered, and he was well taken care of. He no longer had to worry about providing for his family, or that life was going to knock him down again. And then Ava Simmons had come to the castle, reminding him of the small fortune he had lost. Reminding him that, but for her father all but robbing him blind, he might still have owned his own farm—that his wife might have still been alive.

Jenny sighed heavily and glanced at Gayle. 'Did Ava know? About her father and the painting, I mean?'

Gayle shook her head. 'We don't think so. I don't think she could have spoken to us, acted like nothing was amiss, if she'd had any idea.'

Jenny nodded thoughtfully. 'I can see why Miss Bingham knew you had no love for the Simmonses. I suppose she kept track of Basil. That's how she knew about it.'

Gayle nodded. 'Not much gets past the old lady, or Elsie for that matter.'

No, Jenny thought. I don't suppose it does. 'But that only gives you a motive for killing Basil Simmons,' she said bluntly. 'Not for killing his daughter, surely?'

Meecham suddenly withdrew his hand from his daughter's strong grip and stood up. 'Of course not,' he said stiffly.

'Why, we had nothing against the girl. Did we, Gayle?' he asked, and looked at his daughter for help.

Didn't he always, Jenny thought, with a sudden mixture of anger and pity.

'No,' Gayle said staunchly. 'Of course we had nothing against her.'

She's lying, Jenny thought instantly. For Gayle's eyes had dropped, unable to meet the cook's own. And Meecham's sudden show of bravado was as false as his words. They were hiding something. They had resented Ava Simmons. Bitterly. Even if she hadn't been aware of it, she had grown up and flourished partly on the proceeds of the Meecham family painting. She had lived a good, easy life in her father's house. A house paid for by Basil Simmond's treachery. They must have resented her. They wouldn't be human if they hadn't.

But did they kill her?

Jenny sighed again and shook her head. 'And to think, only yesterday I was mourning the fact that nobody had any motive for killing Ava.' She spoke her thoughts out loud. 'Now, everyone does. Roberta and Malcolm could have resented her meddling, although that's a motive so weak I think we can discount it altogether. Elsie could have been jealous. And now you, too, have a good reason to want revenge.' She shook her head. It was all too much. 'Well, at least Janice is out of it all,' she consoled herself, and saw Meecham suddenly jerk, as if someone had just pulled an invisible string.

She glanced up quickly. 'Isn't she?' she demanded sharply.

Meecham stared back at her, then jumped again, as Gayle said, equally sharply, 'Father?'

Meecham collapsed back into his chair, unable to

withstand the onslaught of two feminine demands. 'I wasn't going to say anything...' he began, then sighed. 'It may not mean...' he trailed off, obviously battling with his conscience.

'I think you'd better tell us,' Jenny said gently, whilst wondering despairingly, now what?

Meecham nodded. 'I suppose it's for the best. That afternoon, when his lordship asked me to search the house, after we saw the dagger, I went to Ava's room, like I said. But I didn't just knock, I opened the door. And I saw...'

He paused, getting the memory straight in his mind. 'There's a mirror, facing the door, as you go in. And in it, I saw the reflection of myself holding the door open, and also someone hiding behind it. Hiding behind the door, I mean.'

'Janice?' Jenny asked glumly.

Meecham nodded. 'Janice,' he confirmed quietly.

ELEVEN

JENNY REACHED FOR a jar of the old cook's preserved pears and opened the lid. She sniffed, suspiciously. She supposed they would be all right. But she was now habitually wary of anybody else's preserves ever since that very tragic incident involving a sultan and his pampered pedigree Persian cat.

She drained the large, juicy pears, silently congratulating the gardener on his skill, and washed and diced them. Next, she laid them out in a huge baking dish with some greengages and a good sprinkling of sultanas. Adding sugar and a dash of brandy, she put it to one side and set about making the short-crust pastry to go on top.

Although she worked methodically and, ultimately, deliciously, she did so automatically. For her thoughts were very much elsewhere. On Meecham, to be exact, and what he had just told her.

Gayle had left to see to Lady Vee and Meecham, no doubt wanting to be alone with his thoughts, had skulked off somewhere, leaving her free to digest this latest revelation.

Would losing the family fortune, so to speak, drive him to kill a relatively innocent party? There was no reason to suspect that Ava Simmons even knew of her father's perfidy, let alone condoned it. And she would have been a child herself at the time of the sale of the Meecham family painting.

No, it just didn't ring true. Now if *Basil* Simmons had turned up stabbed to death by a dagger, then yes. But Ava?

Jenny rolled out the pastry with a marble rolling pin—she never used one of the wooden ones, pastry needed the cold strength of marble behind it—and sighed. And what was all this about Janice? She could think of no good reason why the parlour maid should have been lurking about in the governess's room, unless on some errand of skulduggery. Could Meecham have been lying? Trying to throw the spotlight onto somebody else? But Jenny really didn't think so. He wasn't that spiteful. She pulled the dish of fruit towards her without really seeing it and laid the pastry on top. Her fingers began to crimp the edges automatically.

She remembered now the way that Meecham had stiffened whenever Janice had said that she had not returned to the castle the afternoon of the murder. So she probably *had* gone to the governess's room. But why? And had Ava Simmons been in her room at the time? Perhaps she had been killed in her room and then moved?

Jenny shook her head angrily. Now she really *was* giving in to flights of fancy. Had there been any sign of foul play in Ava Simmons's room, Inspector Bishop would have been on to it like a bloodhound.

She looked down at her pie, admiring the dome-shape and crammed-full dimensions. She liked her fruit pies to be *fruit* pies. Not all air and pastry pies. But, as she stared down at the pleasing domed top of the pie and the anaemic-looking, uncooked pastry, a small frown furrowed her brow. For a second she couldn't think what was wrong. But her brain was sending out urgent signals that *something* definitely was. Then it hit her. The pie was only supposed to rise like that *after* it had been cooked.

She spotted the pear-and plum filled bowl still sitting in the centre of the table, and staring down in consternation at the pastry-covered dome, she sighed.

Carefully un-crimping the pastry from around the sides she lifted it off Henry who stared up at her, his small, bulging eyes twinkling. He'd managed to grab a piece of the pastry before it had all been lifted fully off him, and now proceeded to chew it with an expression of complete distaste on his reptilian face.

With a long-suffering sigh, the cook hoisted the pastry-munching tortoise off the table and onto the floor and watched it slowly head for a sunny corner. But she didn't have any high hopes of it staying there. One day, she was sure, his lordship and Lady Vee were going to tuck into a dish and find a nicely baked Henry underneath.

And protesting her innocence wouldn't.... Just then Janice returned, cleaning cloths in her hand, her face flushed with sweat and hard work. 'That's the hall floor done. Phew! It takes me and the dailies who come in hours to do it, but it looks so nice when it's waxed and polished. Of course, the tourists will only dirty it again.'

'Yes, I imagine so,' Jenny said neutrally, washing

her hands and then setting about making some fresh pastry. 'Tea?'

'Oh please. Everybody else is going through his or her movements on the day…you know…with that policeman. He's cornered poor Lady Roberta and Malcolm. Next he's got Meecham and Gayle lined up. He wants them to do exactly as they did on that afternoon. I don't know what he thinks it'll all prove,' Janice continued chattily. 'That sergeant of his is hanging around with a stopwatch, and scribbling away in that notebook of his. It fair gives me the creeps. 'Course, Lady Roberta loves it. A bit of a lark for her, I suppose. No, that isn't altogether fair,' Janice corrected herself studiously. 'She's dead determined to help the police catch whoever it was.'

'Yes, Lady Roberta has a very keen sense of justice,' Jenny agreed, pouring out some tea for the maid and looking for an opening. 'Youngsters usually do. It's only when they get older that they get more cynical. Teenagers just *feel* things more, I suppose.' Which, Jenny thought grimly, was both a good and a bad thing.

'Ah well. I suppose the police have to do their job. I'm just glad I'm well out of it, I can tell you,' Janice said, sitting down and pushing her corn-coloured locks off her forehead in an unconsciously sexy gesture that would have had any man watching drooling in pleasure.

'Yes. Well, I'm not quite sure that that's the case, are you, Janice?' Jenny said, ever-so-mildly. 'I mean, Meecham did see you in Ava's room shortly after he discovered her body.'

'What?' Janice gulped, her voice rising and choking, so that it came out in a strangled gurgle. Her face flushed red then paled into a colour resembling the discarded pastry on the table.

Which reminded her—she'd have to get a move on with making that fresh pastry, Jenny thought absently. Drat that tortoise.

'He saw you, I'm afraid,' Jenny carried on gently, never losing her train of thought even as she mixed flour and butter and sugar together. All the time, Janice continued to stare at her wordlessly.

'I don't know what you mean. Honestly, I don't,' she said eventually, totally unconvincingly. Jenny added cold water to her pastry and mixed and waited.

Janice stared petulantly at the new cook, and decided to get angry. 'What business is it of yours, anyway? You're always poking your nose in. Just because—'

'Janice, I think you'd better calm down,' Jenny said firmly, overriding the other girl's growing indignation. 'If Meecham tells the police what he told me, they could be here at any time, demanding that you tell them what's going on. And they won't stand for any of this waffle,' she warned grimly.

Janice's pretty little chin began to wobble and her lovely blue eyes began to brim. Jenny sighed deeply. 'Janice, why don't you tell *me* what happened? Then it'll be easier to face the police when they ask.'

'But you'll believe me,' Janice wailed, illogically, 'and they won't.'

'Why on earth not?'

'Because they're *men*!' Janice spat out, her eyes flashing with electricity now.

Jenny, pastry made, sat down and leaned back in her chair. 'Ah,' she said flatly. 'Danny.'

Janice flushed. Her lower lip pouted then wobbled, then firmed. 'Oh all right,' she sighed petulantly. 'Like I said, I was supposed to meet him. I said he didn't show up and I went into town shopping. Or did I say I went to the pictures?' Jenny didn't bother commenting. 'Well, the truth is, he *did* meet me. He was waiting at the bottom of the hill, but he said it was the last time. He said he wanted a real woman. That was how he put it. As if I weren't good enough for him!'

She broke off, her sneer not quite managing to keep up with her pain. She looked down at her hands, surprised to find them gripping her mug so tightly.

Jenny added another spoonful of sugar to it and stirred. 'Drink it all up, there's a good girl,' she said solicitously, then carried on smoothly, 'And what did you say to this nice little speech of his?'

Janice laughed, but it was a forlorn sound. She obediently drank some tea. 'Well, I didn't know what to say at first. He sort of…floored me, you know?'

Jenny didn't, but nodded anyway. She herself would never let a man get into a position to 'floor' her.

'So I asked him, why? You know, the way you do,' Janice said earnestly. 'And he said that he wasn't a lad any more. He had his future to think about. He was in a dead end job, he said, and he wanted something more out of life. Well, I knew right away what he was getting at, didn't I? So I said to him, "You just want to live off a well-to-do woman, you do", and he got all angry. Well, then I got angry as well. I started teasing him, like.'

Janice paused to sniff, but as the cook made no accusing or encouraging noises, sniffed again and carried on. 'I said I knew all about his little crush on Lady Roberta's governess. I laughed and said that everyone knew, and was laughing at him behind his back. I said Ava didn't even know he existed, and if she did, she would have been downright offended if he'd asked her out.'

Janice paused, and Jenny sighed. She had a strong suspicion that Janice's narrative had been watered down a bit, no doubt in deference to her genteel ears. 'I see,' she said. And did. In short, they'd had a good old-fashioned barney.

If Danny really *had* thought he could make a play for Ava Simmons, what on *earth* had been going through his head? No doubt he had his greedy handsome little eyes on the Giselle Gallery. After all, Basil had only the one child to leave it to, and he must be getting on in years. No doubt Ava would have inherited it, had she lived. Which meant that Ava's husband would have been set for life.

It wouldn't occur to him that he knew nothing about art, let alone business. But then, he wouldn't have needed to, Jenny corrected herself instantly. Ava had had enough brains for both of them. This, Danny had probably understood instinctively. But then, Jenny thought with a wry twist of her lips, Ava would have had too much sense to ever fall for a man of Danny's dubious charms.

She vividly recalled her first day at the castle, when Danny had offered Ava a ride on his motorbike. She'd been coolly amused and completely uninterested. And Danny, the foolish oaf, had chucked a perfectly nice girl like Janice in pursuit of a dream that would never, in a million years, have materialized.

'Well, I suppose it was for the best that you saw him in his true colours before things went too far,' Jenny said prosaically, and murmured consolingly when Janice burst into tears. The cook reached into her apron and produced a clean handkerchief, and let the wretched girl alone until she'd cried herself out. Then she made some fresh tea.

'Now then. I think you should tell me why you were in Ava's room, don't you?' she said firmly, squarely meeting the maid's eye.

Janice nodded meekly. The tears had obviously wrung her out and she had no fight left in her. 'I went to her room to hide my brooch in her things,' she said flatly, not even recognizing the incongruity of her own words.

'Your brooch?' Jenny repeated, totally wrong-footed.

Janice nodded. 'I wanted to get back at her, you see. For taking away my Danny.'

Jenny opened her mouth to tell the poor, silly girl that Ava had done no such thing, then promptly shut it again. 'And you thought what, exactly?' she prompted gently.

'Well, I planned, the next day like, to say that I couldn't find it. My brooch, that is. It's the only good bit of jewellery I have.'

Jenny looked dubiously at the object in question. Janice was back to fingering it, which at least explained her preoccupation with it throughout the last few days.

It was a simple, silver ballerina, with sparkling rhine-stones for the tutu. It was slightly garish but pretty enough. And, of course, Ava Simmons wouldn't have been caught dead wearing it.

'Er, yes,' Jenny said. 'Go on.'

'Well, I meant to make a big fuss. Like Elsie did about that knitting needle of hers. Go on and on, like she does, whenever she loses something. Except, of course, my brooch wouldn't turn up down the side of a cushion or anything, like Elsie's knitting needle prob-ably will. I was going to insist on searching everyone's room for it. Not that I'd do it, of course. I'd start with Ava's room, and there it would be. See?'

The cook did see. It was pathetic. Everyone would have seen through it in an instant.

'And then they'd have given her the sack, right?' Janice continued, her blue eyes watering again. 'But I didn't know she was dead, did I?' she wailed, her voice rising to a forlorn shriek. 'I didn't know the poor g-girl was l-l-lying dead downst-st-stairs!' she hiccupped, and set off on a fresh bout of weeping.

Jenny walked around to her and patted her shoul-ders awkwardly.

'I've been feeling so guilty ever since,' Janice snif-fled, feverishly twiddling her brooch. 'It was so aw-awful of me. Do you think Ava would forgive me? I mean, if there's a heaven, or whatever?'

Jenny looked down at the wretched blue eyes and felt touched by their simple pleading. 'Yes,' she said firmly, and with infinite kindness. 'I'm sure Ava has already forgiven you, Janice.'

And Janice, hearing the surety in the cook's voice, believed her. Jenny Starling was the sort of woman you always believed meant what she said. But Janice carried on crying for a long, long time nevertheless.

JENNY SLEPT BADLY. Her dreams were haunted by Janice's guilt and the Meechams' misery. She was chased through the night by the spectre of Ava Simmons, the beautiful Munjib dagger lodged in her heart, calling out for help. For justice. For revenge.

She awoke late, sweating and unhappy. She looked at her clock, saw it was past eight, and leapt up, washing and hastily dressing. She ran to the kitchen, expecting reproaches and angry sighs, but found instead Bishop, all on his own, cooking sausages. She looked around questioningly. 'The others?'

'Not hungry,' Bishop said, with a grin. 'They took one look at me and decided to skip breakfast. Can't think why.'

Jenny quickly set about making porridge. It would stall their nibs until she had the main breakfast ready. She was relieved to see Bishop had a panful already on the go. Bacon and eggs would only take a few more minutes.

Meecham came and transferred the bubbling porridge to a silver dish, gave the policeman a reproachful glance as he did so, and left without speaking a word.

'I hear you had them going through their paces yesterday,' Jenny said conversationally, taking over the cooking and watching the bacon crisp up.

'And much good it did me,' Bishop grumbled, lean-

ing against the side of the sink and looking almost
human. 'As far as I can see, Lady Roberta and the art
tutor are out. I can't see Lady Roberta lying for him,
and she insists they were in the music room together
all the time.'

Jenny nodded in agreement. 'No, I can't see Lady
Roberta providing anyone with a false alibi. Not even
for the love of her life.' But she was frowning.

Bishop didn't seem to notice. 'The Meechams now,
either one could have done it. Father wouldn't snitch
on daughter, or vice versa. But they have no motive.'

Jenny bit her lip. Her frown deepened.

'The parlour maid is out of it. Several people saw
her in town on the afternoon of the murder, and again
she had no motive.'

By now, Jenny's frown was making her face ache.

'And Elsie; you're sure she never left the kitchen except for that one time?'

Jenny nodded. 'I'm sure,' she said firmly.

Bishop sighed. 'We went over the timing again. The
fruit cellar is just along the corridor from the conservatory. She could have done it—at a pinch,' he added
honestly. 'But we're no further forward,' he continued
gloomily. 'This afternoon I've asked his lordship, his
wife, and the colonel and his wife to replay their own
actions. I don't suppose that will help either, but you
never know.'

'So you're no further forward than yesterday?' she
commiserated, cracking in some eggs and standing back
as the frying pan spat at her in spite. She sighed deeply.
It had to be done. Even if it made her feel like a prize

tell-tale. Murder was murder. And withholding evidence was a criminal offence.

'I think you'd better sit down, Inspector,' she said quietly and, as he gave her a quick glance, full of suspicion, she said softly, 'About those motives....'

Quickly and concisely, she told him what she'd learnt. Bishop listened, first in growing anger, then in growing respect. When she'd finished he was silent for a long while and then nodded.

'I'll have to get all this confirmed, of course,' he said. 'And I suppose I'd better call in and have a word with Mr Basil Simmons. One way or another, his sins seem to be wrapped up in all this.'

Jenny couldn't agree more. 'So, that's all I have,' she said glumly. 'And you have nothing? All these possible motives are interesting, but hardly helpful. We have no real clues,' she said in frustration.

'Oh, I wouldn't say that,' Bishop said smugly, and the cook glanced at him quickly.

'Oh?' She hated being kept in the dark.

'The Lady Beade School,' Inspector Bishop said, enjoying his momentary sense of power 'have never even heard of Ava Simmons. Let alone offered her a job.'

Jenny stared at him. 'I don't get it,' she said blankly.

The inspector's sense of power vanished. His face collapsed. 'Well, neither do I,' he admitted. 'It seems like a stupid practical joke. I mean....' He went on to curse all practical jokers, but Jenny wasn't listening. Because the cook had suddenly 'got it' after all. And the inspector was wrong: it wasn't a practical joke at all, but a serious attempt to get Ava Simmons dismissed.

Suppose Ava had taken the letter at face value? She'd have handed in her notice, and by the time she'd learned that The Lady Beade had no intention of offering her such a prestigious post, it would be too late. She could hardly go back to their nibs and ask for her job back. It would be too embarrassing.

And who wanted Ava out?

Elsie, of course, but Elsie didn't have the sophistication to write such a letter. Whoever had planned it must have had some special-headed notepaper printed up. One with The Lady Beade address embossed at the top. And the letter must have been typewritten.

No, this was the work of a cold, clear, clever head. It was the work, Jenny was convinced, of Gayle Meecham.

Jenny jumped as Meecham himself appeared by her side, and she felt absurdly guilty. After all, *they'd* been the ones pulling such a dirty trick. She had nothing to reproach herself with. Then she saw Bishop looking at him speculatively, no doubt thinking about the painting he'd sold to Simmons, and felt guilty all over again.

She pulled herself together, dished out the family's breakfast, thanked Meecham stiffly as he relayed Lady Vee's appreciation of some fine porridge, and watched him go.

So that was what all that whispering between father and daughter over in the corner had been about, she thought grimly. Meecham and Gayle had probably posted the letter that first day Jenny had arrived, it would arrive stamped and authentic-looking, all ready to give Ava Simmons such a pleasant surprise the next morning.

But after the murder, Jenny thought, with a little bit of justified satisfaction, they must have been in a real flap. If the letter fell into the hands of the police, they'd find out that it was a hoax. And if it could be traced back to them, it would put them right in the spotlight.

Janice had her brooch.

The Meechams had their letter.

'Fools!' Jenny said angrily, and then smiled at Bishop who gaped at her questioningly.

'Practical jokers,' she said faintly. 'Would you like some fried bread with that, Inspector?'

COLONEL ATTLING WALKED steadfastly past the Munjib dagger without so much as glancing its way. Behind him, Lord Avonsleigh understood his feelings precisely. In fact, the whole group, consisting of the Avonsleighs, the colonel and his lady, Bishop and Myers, studiously avoided looking at the dagger that was now back from the labs, cleaned, and hung back in its original place, for the purposes of this trial run. Of course, it would have to be kept as evidence, for when the time came for a trial.

If the time came for a trial.

Avonsleigh wondered if he ought to sell it. It gave a person the creeps, walking past it like this.

'So, this is where you paused, and admired the, er, dagger,' Bishop was saying. 'What then?'

'The clock struck three,' his lordship said, wondering if all this was necessary, but willing to go along with anything at all that might help. He would have to call in on Mr Basil Simmons soon. Offer his condolences and all that. A chap had to do the right thing. But he was not looking forward to it. Meeting a man whose daughter had been murdered whilst under your roof was not something easily done.

'Right, the clock,' Bishop said, and they all turned to look at the large, rather splendid, eighteenth-century British timepiece. 'Then…?'

'We all went onto the terrace,' Lady Vee said, standing close to her friend, who was beginning to look a little green around the gills. Mrs Attling smiled at her gamely and stiffened her British upper lip.

They all trooped obediently onto the terrace, where they took their original places. Bishop raised the sunshade, as it had been raised on that day (though it was cloudy now) and made sure everyone was sitting in exactly the same places.

The inspector himself drew up another chair and sat just slightly behind Lady Vee.

The conservatory was in plain view only a few yards away. In fact, its lush foliage and spectacular orchids made it a natural focal point of attention.

'And you talked about general things. Mrs Attling, you admired an orchid, I believe?' Bishop said, trying to relax the atmosphere, which had grown suddenly tense.

'Yes. Er, that one there. Of course, it wasn't quite as far out in bloom as it was a few days ago,' Mrs Attling said, pointing out the flower in question. Everybody looked at the conservatory. Bishop nodded to Myers. Myers smartly nipped across the terrace and went through the sunroom, ignoring Meecham who was hovering, waiting to play his part in the drama. In the butler's hand was a tray, but no food. Even Bishop hadn't demanded that much authenticity.

In the hall Myers nodded to a young woman police

constable who walked into the conservatory, standing on the very spot marked on the floor where Ava Simmons had met her death. Next, he walked up to her and touched her. The policewoman obediently lay down on the floor, careful to keep her skirt modestly covering her knees.

Myers looked up. And gaped. He had a clear view across the lawn. In fact, he could pick out in every detail of the scene on the terrace, right down to the colour of the jug on the table, for less than twenty feet separated them. On the terrace, Myer's own dismay was echoed on the faces of everyone at the table.

'But that's…I mean, we could see everything,' his lordship spluttered.

'I don't understand,' Lady Vee said faintly.

Bishop could feel a cold fist of panic strike his gut, but he cleared his throat, swallowing it down. 'Perhaps it is because we were looking at it too obviously. Er, talk between yourselves. Let your eyes roam around the garden a bit. Er, Lord Avonsleigh, turn your head to talk to Mrs Attling,' Bishop recommended, and gestured to Myers to start again.

Obediently, the policewoman rose and the two departed. The scene was played out again. But again, it was obvious to everyone on the terrace just what was going on in the greenhouse. Even his lordship, who was sitting at the most disadvantageous angle, being almost at a right-angle to the conservatory, caught the movement out of his peripheral vision and turned to look.

Lady Vee, Mrs Attling, and the colonel, who were all, in varying degrees, practically facing the greenhouse, couldn't help but look up when Myers and the policewoman re-entered the conservatory. The movement was naturally eye-catching.

And hadn't Miss Simmons been wearing a white blouse, Lady Vee thought in some consternation? That would have been even more obvious than the navy-blue uniform of the policewoman and Myers's own dark suit.

'I just don't see how we could have missed it.' She was the first to speak, after Bishop had had them all go through it a third time.

'And all your chap did just now was touch her on the shoulder,' the colonel pointed out. 'On the day, the murderer must have actually stabbed the poor woman. Wouldn't it have been even more…well…obvious? How could we have sat here and not seen it?' he asked, his voice wavering in disbelief.

Avonsleigh stared at him. Then at his wife, who, for the first time since their marriage, looked totally bewildered. And the fact that Vivienne Margaret was all at sea made him break out in a cold sweat. He looked at Bishop.

Bishop looked at him.

They all looked at the conservatory.

But no matter how many times Myers went through it, and no matter how they arranged the chairs, it always came out the same.

They must have seen the murder.

But they hadn't.

They hadn't!

TWELVE

JENNY SAT BACK in the heavily brocaded chair and stared at Lady Vee.

She stared back. At her feet, the dog snuffled in his sleep, his paws twitching. He had treed a particularly smelly squirrel and was having a high old time. Her ladyship ignored his odd wuffle and continued to stare at her cook, who was developing a faraway look in her eye. She'd just finished bringing Jenny up to date on their afternoon's extraordinary discovery on the terrace.

'And Inspector Bishop tried every angle?' Jenny asked at last, and Vee nodded vigorously.

'We did everything but actually sit with our backs to the conservatory. I just don't understand it.'

'Damned odd,' Lord Avonsleigh said. For once he was book and newspaper-free, and he looked faintly undressed, just sitting there.

'On the day of the murder,' Jenny said cautiously 'had the gardener put anything in the conservatory? Some large plants? Big ferns. Boxes, anything of that kind?'

Lady Vee shook her head. 'A clever idea,' she said thoughtfully, 'but no. I would have remembered. The conservatory was just the same today as I remembered it that awful day. And believe me, I've gone over that afternoon many times in my mind. I'll ask Seth, mind, just to make sure but….' she shook her head firmly, her jowls wobbling. 'No, I'm sure there was a clear view when Miss Simmons was killed.'

'And you definitely saw nothing?' Jenny probed delicately.

'Nothing.'

'Not a sausage,' his lordship confirmed mournfully. The dog, responding to the word 'sausage' even in his sleep, gave a yearning sigh.

Baffled, Jenny shook her head. 'Nothing caught your eye I suppose? Elsewhere in the garden, I mean. You didn't look away at anything at any time while you were out there? A passing kingfisher, perhaps, or a squirrel, a stray cat—anything that might have caught your undivided attention and take it away from the conservatory for a few seconds?'

Lady Vee thought long and hard before replying. 'Again, Miss Starling, it's a good idea, but I can't remember anything of that kind. George?'

He shook his head and sighed. 'No. I'm sure there was nothing. We just sat and chatted. There's no getting away from it, I'm afraid,' he said grimly. 'That poor girl was killed right under our noses and we didn't see a thing.'

Jenny shook her head firmly. 'No, my lord. That's simply not possible.' Her voice was hard and flat, and both glanced at her in surprise.

Jenny noticed and smiled faintly, but her backbone was stiffening. 'If something's impossible, it's impossible,' she said flatly, 'and that's that. Ava Simmons couldn't have been killed without your seeing her, so she wasn't. That's the only way to think of it. To do otherwise is playing right into the killer's hands. You can't give him or her that advantage.'

Lady Vee felt a not unpleasant chill flash across her skin. Although she'd asked her cook to be her eyes and ears, she hadn't truly, in spite of her 'experience', expected Miss Starling to be able to actually *do* anything. Suddenly, listening to the determination in the cook's voice, she knew she'd been mistaken: Jenny Starling *had* caught murderers before, and now she could see why. And how. She glanced at her husband, who met her eye, and nodded.

He had felt it too.

For the first time since the awful incident, Lady Vee began to see light at the end of the tunnel. 'But Miss Simmons *was* killed in the conservatory,' she said, frustration and puzzlement making her voice even louder than usual.

'She was *found* in the conservatory, yes,' Jenny corrected. 'But if none of you saw her killed there....'

'You think her body was moved?' Avonsleigh said flatly. 'But the police found no evidence of it.'

'No. But we already know that our killer is a very clever killer indeed, don't we?' the cook said softly. 'Our killer has been, perhaps, too clever for his or her own good. At least, that's what we must hope for.'

'But the blood on the floor,' his lordship said. 'I had a word with one of those lab boys before they left. They explained that after death, bleeding stops slowly. And they found a lot of blood on the conservatory floor.

Even if the killer *had* killed her somewhere else, then carried her to the conservatory, he must have done it fairly quickly after killing her. And then we'd have seen him do it. Back to square one again. Not to mention the fact that he'd have got blood all over him, and probably left a trail on the floor, leading right back to where the deed was actually done. But Meecham located everyone fairly quickly—too quickly for the killer to have bathed or change, one would have thought. Or wipe up his mess.'

Jenny sighed. 'It *is* a puzzler all right,' she agreed mildly.

Lady Vee, surprised by the quietness of the observation, looked at her quickly.

'You don't sound very angry, Miss Starling,' she observed, a trifle timidly, lest she upset her.

But she needn't have been so wary. Jenny merely smiled at her. 'Oh, I don't get angry, my lady. Or at least, I don't *stay* angry for long. It clouds the thinking, you see. And this case is going to need a lot of thought. Which reminds me, would you mind giving me the address of that gentleman who called who was expecting to see Ava?'

'Of course,' Lady Vee said at once. 'Mr Anthony Grover. I know I asked him for it. I was going to call in one day and see how he's getting along. It was a bit of a shock for the poor old chap, I'm afraid, to come expecting to see a friend, and learning instead.... Quite. But I don't think he'll be able to help you much. Inspector Bishop asked him all sorts of questions at the time, and nothing seemed to come of it.'

Jenny hid a smile. 'Yes, I'm sure Inspector Bishop was very thorough. But I can't help but think that Mr Grover might know more than he thinks he does. Besides, Inspector Bishop's style of questioning and mine are very different. You just never know. And,' she added wryly, 'it's not as though we are swimming in clues, is it? Anything at all might be helpful at this point.'

'True. Beggars can't be choosers,' Lady Vee concurred, rooting in her bag and coming up with the address. Anthony Grover lived in small village not far from Weston-on-the-Green. The cook copied it onto her notepad with a smile.

'Thank you. Believe me, if Mr Grover does have some useful knowledge, albeit unknowingly, I'll find it out.'

Lady Avonsleigh again felt that shiver of coldness cross her skin, and wished the killer of Ava Simmons had been there. If he or she could have heard the cook speak, and seen the glint in her eye—well, the killer would not be feeling so very smug now, of that she was sure.

'I just hate the thought of someone in the castle gloating,' she confided, her voice very angry indeed. 'And with this dinner party tonight, I really don't know how I'll manage.'

'You'll manage, m'dear,' his lordship said placidly. 'You always do.'

'Humph. Speaking of which, how is it all going, Miss Starling?'

The cook smiled, relieved to be back on familiar ground. 'I'm starting with asparagus soup—full of iron and vitamins for your hypochondriac, but a melon boat for the one who's allergic to greens; followed by eels in potato cases—that's with mushroom catsup and lemon juice, of course. Then whole baked trout. Good for both the hypochondriac, as fish is good brain food, and the man who can't eat fat. I have small individual venison pies, again good for the man who can't eat fat as venison has the least fat of all the meats. For the poor unfortunate who doesn't like greens I've done a special vegetable dish adapted from an Italian recipe of non-green varieties—a stew of carrots, black-skinned aubergines, marrows, tomatoes, swede, some horesradish for a bit of bite, potatoes, the white part of leeks and turnips. It's all seasoned lightly with garlic (good for the blood—again you might mention that to the hypochondriac) and simmered to be not too mushy, not too hard.'

She paused for breath, and Vee clapped her hands. 'Wonderful. Fish for brain food, venison for low fat, garlic for the blood, and no greens. I hope I shall remember all that. Oh, Miss Starling, you are a treasure.'

'What's for pudding?' asked his lordship promptly, who could always be relied upon to get his priorities right.

THAT EVENING, ROBERTA joined them in the kitchen, her face alive with curiosity. She watched the new cook attentively, hovering over her as the final countdown to the dinner began. She loved the atmosphere in the castle when her grandparents entertained, and she'd always liked to watch the previous cook at work. The old dear had always seemed to work on the point of nervous breakdown, and without fail, afterwards, had always complained that she was getting too old for this sort of thing.

Eventually, of course, she really *had* become too old, because she'd retired. But Miss Starling, Roberta soon realized, was a whole different kettle of fish. Oh, the excitement was the same, there was the same sense of bustle; Elsie was rushed off her feet, and the stove seemed to be over full with bubbling pots of sauce, simmering vegetables and mouth-watering aromas. But Miss Starling had everything under control. There were no last minute panics. She didn't wail, like the old cook had, that she'd forgotten this or burnt that.

Now, watching her sprinkle almonds over the rows of sizzling trout before putting them back for a final baking, she said forlornly, 'I wish the police would tell me what's going on,' and pouted.

Her petulance was a little spoiled by the eager sniff she made as Jenny lifted the lid off the vegetable dish and the enticing smell of garlic and herbs wafted past her nose.

'I daresay they think you have enough to cope with,' Jenny said mildly. 'What with your studies and your painting and now this dinner.'

Roberta laughed. 'Huh!' she agreed disgustedly. 'And I'd rather eat here tonight anyway. Gramps invites the *dullest* old farts to his dinner parties.'

The kitchen was mostly empty. The others, in deference to the cook's need for space and peace in which to work, wouldn't file in until it was time to actually eat. All the staff loved it when the castle entertained, of course, because it meant that they too enjoyed the feast, albeit downstairs. And they had all, at various times and displaying various skills, pumped her for information on the menu.

Meecham was particularly fond of eels, she'd learned, and Janice had a liking for venison. It was, she'd said, posh food. The sort she never got to eat anywhere else. No doubt they were all scattered about, just counting down the minutes. Meecham would show up soon, since he, Janice and Gayle were all going to help transport and serve the food. But at the moment, only Roberta and Elsie were there, Elsie helping, Roberta actively hindering.

The young lady sat on the side of one of the work units, her long legs swinging, heels tapping on the cupboard doors in a most annoying way. She had, at least, discarded her filthy paint-smeared smock and was wearing a dress that was becoming just a little too small for her. She licked a spoon that she'd filched from the table and her face wrinkled in disgust. 'Ugh, asparagus,' she shuddered and threw the spoon into the sink.

Jenny sighed. 'Don't you have anything better to do, Lady Roberta?' she asked, without much hope.

Although she might appear the epitome of control, she, like all great cooks, suffered from nerves. Were the eels done enough? There was nothing worse than badly cooked eels. Did the soup need more flavouring? Asparagus could be bland, and Lady Roberta's 'ugh' didn't bode well. Underneath, of course, she knew everything was perfect, but still....

'No, as a matter of fact, I don't,' Roberta said unhelpfully. 'I was trapped by that Inspector Bishop again today. Really, it's becoming so boring. He keeps asking the same old questions, over and over again. Was I sure at what time I got to the music room, and I was. Was I sure that Malc never left, and I am. Could I be mistaken about this, that or the other. Today, it was "was Malc acting strangely?"'

Jenny, staring at the vegetable dish, wondered if the marrow had taken on a slightly greenish hue, or was it just her imagination. 'Hum? And was he?' she asked, wondering if she oughtn't to put in just a dash of lemon juice, just in case. Lemon juice would whiten it up, but what about the acidity?

'No, of course he wasn't,' Roberta said scornfully, unaware of the cook's dilemma. 'He was the same as always. He wandered around, like always. He never can keep still. He was fingering a pot of red paint, just like he always plays with his paint pots. He's always fiddling with brushes and things too. I swear he keeps a whole shopload of stuff in that smock of his. I really don't think, you know,' she added seriously, 'that Inspector Bishop has a clue as to what's going on,' Roberta said, youthful scorn and disappointment rife in her young voice.

And that makes two of us, unfortunately, Jenny thought morosely.

Perhaps just a dash of lemon juice.

UPSTAIRS THE GUESTS began to arrive. Lady Vee, her back to the wall, figuratively speaking, had brought out the big guns. She was wearing a full velvet evening gown and dripped diamonds so huge they made the chandelier cringe. By her side, his husband stood in stalwart support.

'Vee, *darling*, how brave of you to carry on like this,' her first guest said, setting the tone.

The rest of the evening was spent, as she had predicted, going over the details in minute, gory detail, satisfying even the most avidly curious. She smiled until her teeth ached, whilst his husband put on such a brave face his jaw felt like it was going to fall off. The food, of course, was superb, and they rounded it all off with a tour of the conservatory.

The evening was, by all accounts, a roaring success.

When it was all over, Vee retired to her bed muttering about ghouls, and Jenny, sat in her now deserted kitchen, muttered about dinner parties. Long into the night, both women lay awake, thinking about the invisible murder of Ava Simmons.

And what they were going to do about it.

ANTHONY GROVER'S HOUSE was typical of that of a retired teacher: small, modest, impeccably neat and rather depressing. Only the garden showed signs of departing from the norm.

Jenny had come in her cherry-red van, which was now parked outside, its resplendent paintwork making it stand out like a sore thumb in the respectable street. Its personalized number plate EAT ME1 didn't do it any favours either.

She stood by the gate, looking around and marshalling her thoughts. The garden was superb. Swathes of colour seemed to flow from one end to the other, following the colours of the spectrum. There was something about it that reminded her of those paintings by Frenchmen—all dabs and impressions of things, and it was then that she recalled that Anthony Grover had been a teacher of art.

Ava's father owned a gallery.

Avonsleigh was famous for its paintings.

'There's an awful lot of art about,' Jenny mused thoughtfully, only just now realizing it. Not being particularly artistically minded herself, she hadn't really thought much about it before. There must be something in it, she thought, fairly. No wonder Malcolm Powell-Brooks loved working at the castle, and was far more interested in keeping his job than in fulfilling that minx Roberta's fantasies.

She opened the gate and walked up to the door, her tread firm. She'd asked Lady Vee before leaving if she would telephone Anthony Grover and pave the way for her, otherwise he might object to a caller out-of-the-blue, nosing into his private affairs. He might even, heaven forbid, think that she was a journalist.

He answered the door after only a few seconds, confirming her assumption that he was expecting her. She was a little unprepared for the fragile, practically wizened figure who stood before her. His shoulders were stooping the stoop of those who suffered from some form of arthritis, and his voice was wavering alarmingly even as he smiled warmly and greeted her. The death of Ava Simmons must have been a hard blow for him.

'You must be Miss Starling. Her ladyship told me you might drop in. Were you a very good friend of Ava's?'

Jenny followed him in to a small sitting-room that overlooked the back garden. It was, if anything, even more beautiful than the front garden. 'I'm afraid not,' she admitted ruefully. 'I hadn't worked at the castle long before it all happened,' she went on, as delicately as possible, and took the seat he offered her.

He left before she could protest, and returned a few minutes later with a tea tray. In the meantime she'd looked around, noting the few but lovely paintings on the walls, and had become the recipient of a large tabby cat's extravagant affections.

'Oh, that's Jemima. I hope you don't mind,' he said, looking down at his cat, which was now firmly curled up on the cook's amply padded lap.

'No, I quite like cats,' Jenny said truthfully, giving the feline a stroke that went from nose-tip to tail-tip, and was rewarded by a loud, extremely satisfied, purr.

'Oh good. Some people don't, you know. Ava wasn't particularly fond of cats.'

Jenny sat up just a little straighter. This was what she was after. Information. Any kind of information. Background. Personality. Anything at all that might help her cast a light on Ava. 'No? Well, some people don't. Didn't she like them as a little girl?'

Anthony Grover shook his head on a smile. 'No, not even then. I lived in Bicester for a long time, practically next door to the Simmonses. That's how we got to know each other,' he explained, settling down into his own chair with some difficulty and an obvious wince. 'Her mother died when she was very young, and her father, well, he worked a lot. Since she went to the local school where I taught, and since she so loved anything to do with art, she got into the habit of coming around to my house, to look at my art books mostly. Sometimes I even took her into Oxford, to the museums. She loved it. She was such a studious little girl.'

'Did she go to university there?' Jenny prompted, although she already knew the answer.

Anthony shook his head. 'I'm afraid not. Not that she wouldn't have been capable, mind you. But her father didn't approve of expensive education for women. He has very strange ideas.'

Jenny didn't miss the grimness in his voice. She waited until he'd poured out the tea and accepted her own cup. 'From what I've heard of Mr Simmons, he's not a very likeable man,' she offered tentatively.

Anthony Grover smiled at her. 'You needn't fence with me, Miss Starling. I may look ancient, but I'm not going to fall apart at the first hint of plain speaking. Basil Simmons, to put it bluntly, is a bastard. Dishonest, cold, ambitious and money-grabbing. He's a social climber of the most odious kind, and a hypocrite to boot. And Ava, of course, was far too intelligent not to have seen it all for herself. Which was why, of course, she left home at the first opportunity.'

'So Avonsleigh was not her first job?'

'Good heavens no, although she was so very happy to be appointed there. Its main reputation is for its paintings, of course,' he added, as if this explained everything. 'When she first arrived, she wrote such long letters to me about touring the castle and practically haunting the corridors in every spare moment she had. She said you never knew what you were going to find next. You went into a perfectly ordinary, barely used room, and there was an El Greco. Or went into the library and got practically assaulted by Gainsboroughs. And then....'

He paused, and took a slow sip of tea. 'And then her letters became less.... I don't know. Less full of life. Less cheerful. I could tell something was wrong. She didn't seem to be getting on with the other staff. I had the impression...I don't know. Not that she was being threatened, or anything like that,' he added hastily, 'but that she was not *happy* about something. She wrote once asking me how I would go about approaching a lord with some bad news. Or how I would ask a lady an awkward question. I got the impression that she wanted to tell them something unsavoury about one of the staff. That there was one who was being more than just unfriendly; but that's only my opinion,' he added hastily, his wavering voice firming for just a moment. 'She never actually came right out and said anything of the kind in her letters, you must understand,' he gabbled, anxious lest he had given the wrong impression. 'I'd have told the police at once if she had. Besides, a nice young constable came around the other day and asked if Inspector Bishop might see them—her letters, I mean. They still have them, as far as I know.'

Jenny took a sip of tea, frowning. This didn't sound good. No, not good at all.

'So you weren't surprised when she wrote and asked you to visit her there? At the castle, I mean?'

'Not really.' Anthony sighed. 'I suppose she'd got into the habit of coming to me in times of trouble.'

'I see.'

'But when I got there, it was already too late,' he added miserably. 'Lady Avonsleigh though, was very kind about it. I'm sure she was very kind to Ava, too. She led me on a tour of the room they were in. She said Ava used to love looking at all the paintings, so she must have taken an interest in her, mustn't she?'

Jenny smiled at him gently and nodded. 'Yes, indeed.' The first time she herself had seen Ava Simmons, she'd been on the staircase, looking at a painting. 'Yes,' she said thoughtfully. Then, more cheerfully, 'Yes, her ladyship is a very kind woman. Did you like the paintings you saw? Perhaps you'd like to come again? I'm sure Lady Vee wouldn't mind if I gave you a tour of the place. They often do have art experts in, you know.'

'Oh, I'd love to,' Anthony said, then his old face creased into a worried frown. 'But I think you'd better ask them first. It might, well, I wouldn't like to embarrass them.'

'But why would you do that?' Jenny asked, surprised.

'Oh, well, you know,' Anthony said, beginning to look distinctly unhappy now. 'It's just that, when I was looking at one of the paintings her ladyship was showing me, I couldn't help but notice that one of them was a copy.'

'A copy?' Jenny echoed blankly.

'Oh yes, it's not uncommon,' Anthony said quickly,

anxious to explain. 'In most of the great families, there were times when one of the sons would gamble away too much money, or made wild speculations on the stock market or something like that. They made a habit of that sort of thing in days gone past. Some sons of noble families all but bankrupted their families at the gaming tables in London. And when that happened, the families would be forced to sell off some assets: silver, paintings, land, that sort of thing. And, in the case of heirlooms and such, they'd have a copy made, so nobody would know. Oh, it's quite common, even amongst royalty,' he continued, falling into teacher mode without even noticing.

Jenny could see that Anthony Grover had been a very good teacher indeed. His voice was alive with enthusiasm. He could make even dry-as-dust history sound interesting.

'All the great houses have histories riddled with naughty sons,' he assured her gleefully. 'The Avonsleighs are no exception, I expect. But, of course, it might embarrass them to have an art buff like myself call in unexpectedly, like the other morning, and well, catch them out so to speak. And I certainly wouldn't want to give that impression, you know,' he added, his old eyes twinkling. 'That I'd caught them out, I mean. It doesn't do to probe too closely into the finances of noble old English castles, you know.'

Jenny hastily agreed that indeed it didn't. Any skeletons their nibs might have, she maintained, should stay firmly locked in the family cupboards. 'But I'll ask her ladyship and arrange for a tour nonetheless,' she added, glad to see the old man's face light up. 'And you can think of nothing else Ava said? Did she ever telephone you?'

'No. She much preferred to write. She said in this computer age of emails and whatnot, that proper letter-writing was becoming a lost art. She was old-fashioned in many respects,' Anthony said, his voice sad and full of pain.

Jenny nodded with a small sigh. She didn't know what else to say. Or ask. She thanked him warmly, rose, and left the old man with his grief.

On her way back, she drove mechanically, lost in thought. If Bishop had found anything even remotely suspicious in Ava's letters to her old mentor, he'd have been on to it by now. So Ava had not made it known which member of staff was giving her so much trouble. But by now, Jenny Starling had a good idea.

And even if she was no closer to solving how the murder was done, she now believed that she had a good base from which to start. But she'd have to be careful. Very careful. As she'd told Lady Vee only yesterday, the killer was clever.

Clever enough to commit an invisible murder, in fact.

THIRTEEN

THE MOMENT JENNY woke up the next morning, she knew she'd heard something important. Not just from Anthony Grover, but from someone else. What was it?

For a long while she lay in bed, trying to remember, without success. Unable to return to sleep, it was barely dawn when she took her bath, but the hot steam did nothing to loosen her mental processes. She'd heard something vital, she just knew it, but it hovered on the fringe of her mind, like a tantalizing butterfly that refused to be netted.

As she dried her hair and dressed, she firmly, if reluctantly, put the matter to one side. There was no point in worrying away at it. She knew from past experience that her subconscious would carry on with the job for her, mulling it over until the answer popped back into her mind like a nicely done piece of toast.

In the meantime, she had work to do.

At some point she would have to have a word with the Avonsleighs. If what she suspected was true, well, it would not be pleasant. There would be a scandal. A fine reputation would take a severe knocking.

Of course, there was always the possibility that she might be wrong. She had not, as yet, any clue at all as to *how* the killer had done the killing. The invisible murder of Ava Simmons still made no sense at all. And everyone had a reasonable alibi.

The killer included.

But, as she set about making breakfast, she knew she was not wrong. A visit to Basil Simmons today was a must. It would tidy things up in her mind. If only she could remember what it was that she'd heard!

Whenever she was uptight, Jenny cooked.

That morning, their nibs were presented with a citrus fruit cocktail, freshly made and pleasantly chilled, then kippers, still sizzling, followed by a home-made museli they'd never heard of, or tasted, before, but which Meecham informed them cleared the palate of the fish for the next course. The full English breakfast followed.

In the breakfast room, Lady Vee leaned back, the final mouthful gone, and said, 'I wonder what's up?'

Her husband, puffing over his last dishful, but determined not to leave a single tomato left unturned, looked up. 'What do you mean?'

She smiled at him warmly. 'You are such a duffer, George,' she said fondly. He smiled. The smile, however, quickly vanished when his wife continued in a quiet, worried, but calm voice, 'I think, you know, that we might hear from Miss Starling today. About the murder.'

'Oh?'

His wife contemplated the delicious feast they'd just eaten, and sighed. 'And I don't think it's going to be good news, George.'

After forty-one years of marriage his lordship was, by now, quite rightly convinced of his wife's infallibility, and his spirits sank. 'I was going to go and see Ava's father today,' he murmured, and his wife shook her head.

'I would leave it a day or two, dear,' she advised, sagely. 'Just in case.'

JENNY HAD NEVER set foot in an art gallery before, mainly because art was most definitely her mother's arena, and she knew better than to even so much as dabble a toe in it.

When she wasn't saving the trees, whales, or whatever else needed saving, Jenny's mother was painting; and painting anything at all that took her fancy. Her daughter's long-suffering van, council walls, park benches—once, even a neighbour's poodle—using body paint of a peculiarly fetching shade of lilac. (The dog's owner *still* wasn't speaking to her.) Consequently, as she drove into Bicester, Jenny firmly thrust aside worrying thoughts about her ignorance of art, and wondered instead if Basil Simmons was going to live up to his seedy reputation. But the fact that he hadn't yet set foot in the castle told its own story, surely? When your daughter is murdered, you'd think most men would at least want to talk to the people involved. Did he simply not care? Or was he playing a crafty game of his own?

She parked behind a Tesco's, straightened her shoulders, and walked into the town centre.

The Giselle Gallery was not hard to find. It occupied a central spot in Sheep Street, the ancient central spine of the town. The tower of St Edbergs—or was it Eckberts? Jenny was unsure—dominated the skyline, and the gallery came a close second. It was an old building, with an imposing façade of well-maintained masonry. It *looked* important. A simple brass plaque off to one side of the door bore the one word *Giselle* in italic script.

To one side of the gallery was a hardware shop, to the other a newsagents. The mundane next to the magnificent looked incongruous, but only served to make the gallery look even more like the *grande dame* that it undoubtedly was. Jenny took a deep breath and walked in, not knowing what to expect.

She'd worked for a very successful modern sculptor once, in a very run-down area of London that he'd seemed inordinately proud of, perhaps because he was the son of a lord. He'd worn his hair long, a beard even longer, and had an unfortunate habit of forgetting to get dressed in the morning, often leaping out of bed naked and starting work immediately.

She had not stayed long.

The nakedness itself didn't bother her much; after all, if he could be brave enough to solder metal with an acetylene torch, sparks flying, whilst stark naked, who was she to be a killjoy? But when she found him using her custard to paint a metal sunflower, and had asked her to make up some gravy so that he could make it look drooped and nearly over—some allegory for something or other—she'd very quickly packed her bags and left.

People who didn't eat merely worried her. People who used food for something other than the purposes of eating, were, in her opinion, quite simply off their trolley.

But this gallery bore no resemblance to anything Jenny could recall from her brief, unhappy stay in Clapton.

She walked into a high-ceilinged room with enormous windows that let in floods of light. The walls were painted a slightly off-white colour that soothed, rather than dazzled, the eye. As she looked around, she was surprised to see how spaciously the drawings and paintings were laid out. She'd expected them to cram the walls. On tall pedestals, stood arrangements of orange tiger lilies. In one corner, a small, dark wooden desk housed a telephone, an old-fashioned pen and ink set, a pile of creamy stationery, and a young man of extremely dapper appearance.

Sergeant Myers would instantly have recognized a soulmate, Jenny thought with some amusement, as he rose and walked or, more accurately, glided towards her. His suit was navy blue, the stripes immaculately thin. His shoes, black, gleamed. His tie, a deep red, glowed like a ruby. His only piece of jewellery was a watch. 'Good morning, madam. May I help you, or are you merely browsing?'

Jenny smiled. 'Browsing. For the moment,' she added. Faced with such a paragon as this, she was not quite sure how to ask to see the owner. She was sure a blunt 'Is Mr Simmons in?' would not go down well. She was, she realized somewhat belatedly, in 'appointment only' territory. And she didn't have one.

'Ah, yes, it's such a pleasure isn't it,' the young man continued, 'to feast your eyes on works of art? As you can see, here at the Giselle we like to give every piece enough room to breathe. There is none of that vulgar showmanship that's unfortunately become so popular in London nowadays. Mr Simmons is most insistent on it.'

'Yes, I'm sure,' Jenny murmured, fighting back a desire to panic. 'His daughter felt much the same way. We were great friends, you see,' Jenny continued, not a blush in sight, 'and she taught me an awful lot about art.'

The young man's face clouded most theatrically. 'Ah, yes, poor Miss Simmons. You er, know what happened?' he probed delicately.

His eyes were running over her almost feverishly. What height! What curvaceous, amply-proportioned form! And those eyes! He could see her in a Rubens painting, a simple white swathe of material draped over her magnificently naked form. He could mentally recreate the blend of skin-tone the great master would use. And her profile.... His rapturous thoughts broke off as the woman turned to him and speared him with those same beautiful eyes. In them was an expression that caused his face to flood with colour.

Jenny watched him, wondering what on earth had made him stare at her like that. He was very nearly drooling. 'Yes, I did know. As a matter of fact, I was wondering if I shouldn't call on Mr Simmons and offer my condolences,' she replied stiffly.

'Oh. Ah, yes,' the young man said, recovering a more normal skin tone. 'Well, I'm not sure that....' His eyes flickered past hers and Jenny was turning sharply before he could even begin to stop her.

Through the large window, looking sideways down the building's façade, she could see a small side door open. It was a door that obviously led exclusively to the upper floors, perhaps even to Basil Simmons's private rooms, for she knew he lived over the gallery. But it was not the layout of the building that concerned her, so much as the figure walking down the steps. A figure she knew very well indeed.

Elsie Bingham paused on the bottom step to unbutton a rather ancient-looking coat that Jenny had never seen before—her Sunday best, probably. Dark blue, with large gold buttons that, even from this distance, looked tarnished and chipping, it had a little white ball of some kind of fur, probably rabbit, pinned to the lapel. But it was not Elsie's attempt at sartorial splendour that caught her attention the most, it was the look on her face.

It was a look Jenny Starling would never forget. It was triumphant. Gloating. Savage. *Happy.*

For the first time in her life, perhaps, Elsie Bingham looked positively happy. Jenny watched her set off up the street, her step for once light and jaunty. Oh Elsie, Jenny thought pityingly. Oh Elsie, *what have you done*?

'I can see he must be free now,' Jenny pointed out with ruthless logic, even as she was wondering what on earth her kitchen maid had been up to.

'Er, yes. Perhaps I should tell him you're here. Mrs…?'

'Miss Starling,' she corrected, giving him another one of those looks that made him blush. He hoped she wasn't a mind reader. But really, she was a walking Rubens or Titian model. He hurried away and a few minutes later came back. He looked puzzled. 'I'm afraid Mr Simmons says he doesn't know you.'

Jenny smiled. 'Go back and tell Mr Simmons that although he may not know me, I do know the identity of the visitor who just left. And while you're at it, you might also tell him that I am employed at Avonsleigh Castle.'

The young man went white, looked as if he might faint, but managed to turn and get himself out of the room. On his way up to Mr Simmons's private rooms he began to shake. Rumour had it that the murderer of his employer's daughter still worked at the castle. The police were also said to be baffled. And to think, he'd been alone in the same room as a murder suspect. And he'd been imagining her naked!

The young man shuddered, and almost fainted again.

A few minutes later, Jenny stood in the same room as Basil Simmons.

The assistant had escorted her up in a most curious way, keeping a distance of at least several yards between them, and always making sure his back was never turned towards her. Since he had mounted the stairs first, that meant that he had gone up sideways, like a crab, his back pressed firmly to the wall. Now he sidled around her and shot out of the door like a petrified rabbit.

Jenny watched him go, astonishment written clearly across her face. 'What on earth's wrong with *him*?' she asked, and a voice, nasal and cold, answered from the heavy shadows in one corner of the room. The office, unlike the gallery below, was poky, dark, and depressing.

'He thinks you might be a killer, I imagine. He doesn't have a great supply of backbone, does Neville.'

Jenny turned abruptly to the shadows, her eyes narrowing. She deliberately said nothing. After a long war of wills, Basil Simmons finally moved, coming out into the light and revealing himself to be a man of average build and height, with normally greying hair, normally ageing skin, and a thin, cruel mouth. His eyes were heavy-lidded and slit. They revealed nothing at all.

But Jenny instantly understood that this man could smile. This man could charm. This man could radiate warmth with as much ease as he was now radiating arctic coldness.

'Mr Simmons,' she said. Then, more softly, 'Yes.'

Something flashed in his eyes. He'd been recognized, his soul analysed and charted, and he didn't like it. He didn't like it one little bit. He moved briskly to a chair in front of a desk and sat down. He indicated the chair in front of him.

'Please sit down, Miss Starling. What can I do for you?'

'Well, you might start by telling me what your daughter was doing here,' she said, not at all fooled, or cowed, by his attempt to dominate the room.

For possibly the first time in his life, Basil Simmons looked surprised. Then his eyes went flat. 'My daughter is dead, Miss Starling, as you must know if you do, indeed, work at the castle.'

'I wasn't referring to Ava,' Jenny said quietly.

Basil glared at her. 'My private life is none of your business.'

'It is when murder has been committed, Mr Simmons,' she shot back. 'According to the police, Elsie had a legitimate motive.' She used the word 'legitimate' deliberately, and was rewarded by a sharply in-drawn breath.

'I do believe, Miss Starling,' he said quietly, 'that you're poisonous.'

'Only when I have to be, Mr Simmons,' she said softly. And smiled.

Basil Simmons stared at her in total surprise. She didn't look like a cobra. She looked fat and harmless and also unexpectedly, but definitely, beautiful. But a cobra she was. And for the first time in his life, he didn't feel so much like a mongoose as a fat, juicy rat.

'What do you want?' he asked abruptly. He wanted this woman out of his house. Out of his gallery. Out of this room. He was sweating now. He didn't like being in the vicinity of someone that he couldn't manipulate, swindle, or intimidate.

'Did you murder your daughter, Ava?' Jenny asked quietly.

'No,' Basil Simmons said shortly.

He didn't, the cook noted with interest, sound sur-prised by the question.

'Do you care that she's dead?'

'Not much. She left home years ago. I haven't seen her since.'

'Have you ever been to Avonsleigh?'

'No.'

'Have you ever sent one of your, er, representatives, on any of the tours of the Avonsleigh art collection?'

Basil Simmons hesitated. 'I have, yes.'

'For what purpose?'

'Curiosity.'

Jenny said nothing for a moment. That was an unexpected twist.

Basil shifted restlessly. 'That's the truth,' he said, with just a hint of panic in his voice now. He had, in fact, been telling her nothing but the truth. He knew instinctively that that was the only way to get rid of her. His palms began to itch.

Jenny continued to look at him thoughtfully. She, too, believed him to be telling her the truth. His answers were much what she expected. But that was not what she had come for.

'Do you want to see the killer of your daughter caught, Mr Simmons?' she finally asked, her tone of voice as mild as milk.

It was Basil Simmons's turn to stare. He licked his lips, which felt as dry as the Sahara. 'I, well, yes. Yes, as a matter of fact, I do. She was *my* daughter. Do you understand?'

Jenny did. Perfectly. Ava had been unloved and almost certainly unwanted, since she'd been born female and therefore not the all-important son. But she *was* his property. She *had* come from his loins. He probably felt miffed that someone had snuffed her out without so much as his permission or say so. But it was enough for her purposes. She nodded and rose. 'If I call and ask you to come to Avonsleigh, will you come, and do exactly what I say?'

At first he felt only a flood of relief that she was going. Then her words penetrated. 'Will it be dangerous?' he asked quickly.

Jenny's lips twisted grimly. 'No, Mr Simmons. At least, not dangerous for *you*.'

Basil Simmons shuddered, quite visibly. 'All right,' he agreed, his voice barely a whisper. 'All right.'

Jenny nodded and left.

Outside, she took a deep breath of cool, clean air. 'What an awful, ugly man,' she said out loud, but luckily no one was within hearing distance. Then she added, sadly, 'Poor Ava.' She was still shaking her head as she turned and headed back to the car-park.

From his poky window, Basil Simmons watched her go. His sweating frame felt cold now. He quickly began to convince himself that he had not really been afraid—that he had always been in control of the situation, but he knew, even then, that when the call came, as he knew it would, he would go to Avonsleigh. And that he would do what she asked of him.

JENNY WATCHED ELSIE all day long.

The kitchen maid did everything but hum. She smiled at Henry, when she found the tortoise in a sack of carrots. She discovered her battered old handbag was missing, but only said it would probably turn up, making even Janice, not the most observant of girls, look at her in some surprise. She even smiled at Malcolm when he sloppily washed out some paint jars in the sink, leaving them to drain on the sideboard and leak pale blue, mint green and sickly yellow stains onto the steelwork.

Dinner came and went. Jenny's bacon clanger, with leeks, was a rousing success, as was her rice and pineapple pudding.

With infinite patience, Jenny waited until they all began to file out of her kitchen. Janice had a date with a new boyfriend at the Jolly Farmer. Malcolm dodged Roberta and fled to his room. Roberta sulked, then went to bed. Meecham and Gayle went to see to their respective charges, Meecham to lay out his lordship's smoking jacket and slippers, Gayle to see to her ladyship's nightly ablutions.

Elsie was halfway into her coat before Jenny finally managed to catch her alone.

'Elsie, can I have a word please?' she asked gently but firmly, and the kitchen maid froze. She recognized the tone at once, and her eyes rounded. Fear came into them.

'It was my morning off, you know,' she said quickly. 'And I peeled them leeks as soon as I got back.'

'I know. It has nothing to do with your work, Elsie.'

Some of the fear left. Elsie continued getting into her coat, but walked reluctantly towards the cook as she did so. 'Yes, missus?'

'Elsie, I went to see Mr Simmons today.'

Elsie went white. 'Oh. Ah. Well, to offer your condolences, like, I expect.'

'Not quite,' the cook said wryly, but let it pass. 'I saw you leaving. I was wondering, to be frank, what had taken you to the Giselle.'

Elsie's face took on a stubborn look. 'Just offering me respects, missus, that's all,' Elsie said. 'I thought someone should do it.'

Jenny recognized the glint in her eye at once, and knew what it meant. Elsie would stick to her story come what may. Unimaginative, down-trodden people, she knew, could be very stubborn indeed when the need arose.

She sighed wearily. 'I see. Well, good night, Elsie,' she said. There was no point in saying anything else now. To pursue it would only make the kitchen maid even more truculent.

A look of relief flashed across Elsie's pinched face before she turned and left. Jenny watched her go, her eyes troubled, for Elsie simply did not have the right weaponry to go up against a man like her father.

She was going to come a cropper if she didn't watch out.

MEECHAM KNOCKED ON the door timidly. His employers had retired to the outer boudoir, a small but cosy room that adjoined their huge bedroom. They often had a nightcap there before retiring to bed. Lady Vee was already dressed in a voluminous nightdress and dressing-gown—his lordship was in his smoking jacket and slippers.

It was nearly midnight.

'I'm very sorry to disturb you,'—Meecham half-bowed to each in turn—'but Miss Starling begs an audience. I did tell her it was very late, but....' He let the sentence finish itself, and missed the speaking look that passed between husband and wife.

'It's quite all right, Meecham,' Avonsleigh reassured his upset manservant. 'Lady Vee and I are quite happy to receive Miss Starling whenever she chooses.'

Meecham hid his look of surprise and withdrew. A

moment later, Jenny walked in. 'I apologize for the lateness of the hour,' she began, but Lady Vee rose with a pooh-poohing wave of her hand and reached for the sherry bottle.

'A nightcap, Miss Starling?'

Jenny rarely drank—well, rarely enough—and she looked at the glass of dark-brown liquid a little apprehensively. Then she remembered what she was here to say, and nodded. 'Yes, please, your ladyship.'

Again a look passed between husband and wife. Both had already ascertained that their new cook didn't so much as make even the odd little foray into the cooking sherry. Their old cook had been apt to make a lot of dishes that required brandy in them. And rum. And cider. So this show of unexpected tippling from someone of Jenny's ilk only confirmed her ladyship's earlier fears.

Jenny took a small sip, wrinkled her lips in distaste, and caught Lady Vee indicating a chair. She sat down and then quickly shot up again. She sighed, removed Henry from the padded stool and, not quite knowing what to do with him, sat down and left the reptile to crawl about on her lap.

She took another sip of sherry, then a deep breath.

'I'm afraid I'm going to have to ask you a rather, well, impertinent question, my lord,' she said, looking at George. 'I hope you won't think it too appalling. But I simply must know the answer.'

She paused, giving him time to make the usual splutterings.

George, however, decided to forgo the usual splutterings and merely glanced at his wife questioningly.

Lady Vee sighed. 'You know who did it, don't you?' she said flatly.

Jenny nodded. 'Yes, m'lady,' she said simply. 'I think I do.'

'And it's bad, isn't it?' Lady Vee said, her booming voice falling to something very near a whisper.

Jenny frowned. 'It's going to be embarrassing,' she said, groping for the right words. 'I'm afraid there'll be a bit of a scandal.'

'A scandal that will be bad for one of us?' Avonsleigh asked, his voice firm and steady.

He'd always, Vivienne Margaret thought fondly and gratefully, been a very good husband to have in a crisis. She reached out for his hand, and grasped it tightly. He'd been her rock in the aftermath of the death of their firstborn son and his wife. He'd been a pillar of strength then, and he was being one now. She squeezed his hand tightly, and felt it being squeezed back.

The cook didn't miss this telling gesture, and she swallowed a sudden lump in her throat.

'It'll be bad for Avonsleigh, yes,' Jenny confirmed, careful with her choice of words. 'But I have to remind you, it's all theory at the moment. I still don't see how the actual murder was done, and until I figure that out, I don't have a chance of proving anything.'

She looked them squarely the eye.

Lady Vee nodded. 'I think,' she said quietly, 'you'd better tell us all you know. Or rather, all that you suspect. And then ask your question.'

So Jenny told them all she knew.

And then she asked her question.

FOURTEEN

INSPECTOR BISHOP PULLED up at the castle, stepping on the brakes so hard that gravel spurted from beneath the car wheels. It had not yet been a week since he'd received that first call saying that there'd been a murder up at the castle, but it felt like a lifetime.

Now, though, he felt as happy as he'd ever been since the whole mess started, for things were moving at last. If the inhabitants of the castle had not seen him around very much recently, they would soon find out why.

'Meecham first, sir, or the girl Janice?' Myers prompted.

'Oh, we might as well start with the butler, I think,' Bishop said, unfolding his frame from the car and taking a deep breath of the morning air. 'Any word from our friend, Miss Starling?' he asked drolly, and Sergeant Myers shook his head.

'Not a peep, sir.'

Bishop caught an undercurrent in his sergeant's voice and glanced across at him. His own lips twisted. 'I know. Ominous, isn't it? But for once, we have the upper hand. So let's go and shake the tree and see what apples fall out,' he said cheerfully.

Meecham showed no signs of strain when he answered the summons to the secondary door. By now, he was used to policemen tramping in and out of the place whenever they pleased. Two constables were always wandering about somewhere, and only their faces changed with every eight-hour shift. 'Good morning, sir. Sergeant,' he greeted them mildly.

'Meecham. Is your daughter around? I'd like a word with you both. In the kitchen, I think,' Bishop said briskly, in such a no-nonsense manner that even Myers felt himself wince.

Meecham's lips tightened, but he showed them into the cavernous kitchen and left to fetch his daughter. By the sink, Jenny was peeling onions. 'Good morning, Inspector,' she said cordially.

Bishop, seeing that they were alone for the moment, walked over quickly. 'What's all this I hear about you visiting Basil Simmons yesterday?' he asked peremptorily, and was forced to cool his heels while Jenny rinsed the onions under the tap and retrieved a rather formidable knife from a drawer before answering.

Instinctively, Inspector Bishop took a step back.

'I thought it might prove to be fruitful,' Jenny said, and began slicing with such speed and dexterity that Bishop watched, fascinated. After only a few moments, however, his eyes began to water painfully, and giving her a sharp look, he sensibly retreated.

'And did it?' he persevered, once he was sitting at a safe distance from the sink.

'I think so, yes.'

Meecham chose that moment to return, saving the cook from a further grilling. But, Bishop vowed

silently, he'd get back to her on that. It had sounded
rather interesting.

'Ah, Mr Meecham. Gayle. Please sit down,' he said,
so jovially that Jenny momentarily stopped chopping.

'Perhaps you'd care to tell us all about your cousin,
Louise,' Bishop said softly, and had the satisfaction
of watching Meecham pale, quite spectacularly. 'You
know, Mr Meecham. The one who works as a secretary
at The Lady Beade School?'

Jenny sighed loudly. Bishop ignored her. Meecham
and Gayle continued to stare at him mutely. They
looked, Bishop thought grimly, like a pair of rabbits
caught in car headlights.

'You see, we found a letter in Miss Simmons's room
offering her a job at the school. But the school said they
made no such offer. When my sergeant took the letter
to them, they were rather puzzled. The letterhead, you
see, was genuine.'

Jenny sighed again, even more loudly. She'd suspected that they'd had the letterhead printed up somewhere, and not that they'd convinced a relative to steal
a sheet of genuine paper. Silly beggars. She only hoped
Bishop wasn't going to be bloody-minded about it. He
was just in the right mood to get the cousin fired from
her position, if rubbed the wrong way.

Meecham coughed. 'I see you've found us out, Inspector,' he said, seeing at once that it was useless denying it. 'But you mustn't blame Louise. We told her it
was for a practical joke.'

'That's right,' Gayle said quickly. 'Louise would have
been very upset if she knew what we'd had in mind.'

'Which was, Miss Meecham?' Bishop asked silkily.

Jenny began chopping furiously. The sound ricocheted around the room, making Myers give her a nasty, sideways glance.

'To get Ava out of the castle, Inspector,' Gayle said, her voice calm and level.

'Because of the painting her father swindled you out of? Oh, yes, I know all about that, too,' Bishop said flatly.

Gayle cast an accusatory look at Jenny's back. 'I see. Well, then, you know it all,' she said flatly.

'Which means, Inspector,' Meecham began, a little too eagerly, 'we're not likely to have killed Ava, when we already had a plan underway to get her out of the castle.'

'Perhaps,' Bishop conceded. 'On the other hand, a very clever person might think that a nice red herring like that would be just the job to throw suspicion off himself or herself. Don't you think so?' he asked craftily, and Gayle actually gasped, for the first time ever, as far as Jenny knew, losing her composure.

'You mean you think that we might have written the fake letter and then killed Ava, knowing that you'd find the letter and believe…?' Gayle's voice trailed off helplessly.

'Just what you wanted us to think? That you'd have no reason to kill her, since you were already in the process of turfing her out?' Bishop finished for her. 'It's very feasible, don't you think, Miss Meecham? You must admit, it does have a certain something.'

Gayle's eyes darkened. It was a phenomenon Bishop

had only seen once or twice before, and it had always sent the hairs on the nape of his neck standing to rigid attention. 'That's insane, Inspector,' she said, her voice as dark as her face.

'Or very clever, Miss Meecham,' Bishop corrected, his voice now like honey. 'And I happen to think you're a very clever person. Perhaps, even, the cleverest person here.'

Jenny couldn't but help admire both his thinking and his perspicacity. Of them all, Gayle *did* have the best brains. Apart from herself, of course. She reached for a pile of chicken breasts and began to remove the skin, going over Bishop's theory in her mind. It was a good one. Meecham and Gayle did have a perverse kind of alibi with that silly letter of theirs. Yes, Bishop was no fool.

'Is that all, Inspector?' Gayle asked flatly, and watched a flash of fury pass over his face. She smiled. 'We admit we faked the letter from the school. We admit we wanted Ava Simmons out of the castle. We don't admit that we killed her, because we didn't. Now, is there anything else?' she repeated, her eyes all but glowing a challenge because she knew the Inspector was powerless. Without clues. Without proof.

And Bishop knew that she knew it.

'No,' he finally snapped. 'There's nothing else. *For the moment.*'

'Good, because I must see to her ladyship. She likes me to do her hair on the days between her professional hairdresser's visits.' Gayle rose and pushed away magnificently from the table.

Meecham, seeing his daughter leaving, quickly rose too, lest the Inspector badger him some more when he was alone and defenceless.

But Bishop had had quite enough of the Meechams. When they'd gone he shot Myers a disgusted look. 'That's one cold woman, Sergeant,' he said, and Myers nodded faithfully in agreement.

Jenny sighed again and Bishop, seeing the onion-torture was over, returned to the sink. 'And what did *you* make of all that, Miss Starling?' he asked smugly, waiting for praise.

'It was interesting,' Jenny conceded. 'But then I already knew that Gayle was a very capable girl. She's had to be, looking after that father of hers. And the fact that she wouldn't be bullied means she's a very unusual girl indeed. I imagine she'd have made an excellent mother superior in the dark ages. Head nuns had immense power in those days, you know—had control of lands and sometimes vast wealth. They were the only women who were allowed such power.'

Bishop stared at her, unprepared for a history lesson. Then, aware that her placid profile showed no signs of surprise, said icily, 'You knew, didn't you?'

'About the letter? Yes, I guessed. About the cousin? No. It was obvious someone at the castle wanted Ava out. Elsie didn't have the brains and Janice didn't have the imagination. That left Lady Roberta, who resented her governess's interference in her little infatuation, Malcolm Powell-Brooks, who might have been worried that Ava's continuing complaints might get him fired from his prize job, or the Meechams. Roberta is too

young to have thought of anything so ingenious and I
doubt Malcolm had ever heard of the school. That left
the Meechams.'

Bishop nodded. 'You make it all sound so simple.
But we've come up with something that even you don't
know about, Miss Starling,' he said, goaded into brag-
ging. 'Myers, bring that pretty little blonde piece down
here.'

Jenny glanced at the inspector as she seasoned the
chicken breasts and placed them in her own special recipe marinade. 'Didn't Janice tell you about her brooch,
Inspector? I thought she had. I told her—'

'Oh, yes, we've gone through all that,' Bishop assured her. 'Meecham admitted lying, or at least, not
telling the whole truth about what happened when he
went to Ava's room the afternoon of her death. A rather
dark horse, Meecham, don't you think?'

Jenny refused to be drawn. She reached for a pile of
mixed herbs and began to defoliate them. The secret
to a good chicken casserole was always in the herbs.

'And Janice confessed to planting the brooch in Miss
Simmons's room,' Bishop continued thoughtfully. 'Isn't
it funny how everyone had something against her and
did something about it, but nobody actually killed her?'
he mused sarcastically.

Jenny's lips twisted into a grim smile. 'Yes. Isn't
it just.'

Janice walked hesitantly into the room, catching the
last few words, and cast the cook a terrified look. Behind her, Myers closed the kitchen door with a firm

whump making Janice jump. Just as she was intended to, of course.

Jenny glanced reprovingly at Bishop, one eyebrow raised.

Bishop ignored her and turned to Janice. 'Now, young lady, I think it's about time you told us about this boyfriend of yours.'

'Barry?' Janice said, caught on the hop and thinking of her latest beau. 'We only went out last night—'

'Not Barry. *Danny*. How many boyfriends do you have, Miss Beale?' he snapped.

Janice blushed. 'I told you. It's all over between Danny and me.'

'Yes, so you said. You also said that when you met Danny the afternoon of the murder, he left on his motor bike after breaking it off with you.'

'Well?' Janice said, clearly getting a little of her spirit back, and raising her chin defiantly. 'He did.'

'He didn't go far,' Myers said abruptly from behind her.

'His motor bike was seen on the other side of the spinney, not a quarter of a mile from here. Our witness said it was there from nearly a quarter to two until four o'clock. Care to tell us what it was doing there?'

Janice flushed. 'How should I know? I'm not his keeper anymore.'

'You didn't see him about? From the window of Miss Simmons's bedroom, perhaps, when you were trying to frame her for being a common thief?' Bishop asked, his voice so conversational it was doubly insulting.

Janice gasped. Jenny sighed again. Loudly.

'No. I never saw him. What would Danny be doing at the castle anyway?' she challenged, but her voice was no longer confident.

'Yes, that's what we wondered,' Bishop said softly. 'As it stands, we're supposed to believe that you and Danny boy had a raging fight and broke up. But we have only your word for that. Don't we?'

Janice stared at him, her mouth going dry. 'What do you mean?' she asked faintly.

'This murder, now, was a very clever murder,' Bishop mused, smiling like a cat at a mousehole. 'You see, Janice,' Bishop said silkily, 'perhaps it was too clever for just one person to commit on their own. Perhaps it took two. And perhaps, to throw us off, these two conspirators pretended to break up. One goes back to the castle openly whilst the other one sneaks in the back way, hiding his motor bike in the woods.'

Janice stared at him. 'But why would we kill her?' she asked, and unintentionally stopped Inspector Bishop dead in his tracks.

Mixing up a chicken stock, Jenny grinned widely. But she was careful to keep it hidden. She reached for some cornflour, and waited. Get out of that, Inspector, she thought wryly.

'Don't think we won't find out, young lady,' Bishop snarled, forced into threats.

Janice tossed her head bravely. 'You know what I think? I think Danny was just doing some poaching. He does that, you know, often. And not just rabbits and pheasants, neither. I was with him once when he borrowed a van from his mate and there was a whole deer in the back....' Janice broke off, aware that, perhaps, she was not doing herself any favours. 'Not that I know where he got it from, of course,' she added hastily. 'He never told me anything about what he got up to. Everybody knows the gamekeeper here complained about somebody having a deer or two, but he's never caught anybody at it,' she finished, in a final flash of defiance. 'He's too clever, is Danny boy. Thinking he might have done something to her,' she muttered darkly. 'He was sweet on her, he was.'

'Yes,' Bishop said, his eyes glittering. 'We know. Or was all that just a ruse too, hmm? After all, Danny made his play for her very obvious. Everyone here knew about it when we asked them. They all thought it was so funny. Danny trying it on with someone like Ava Simmons. He didn't have a hope, did he?' Bishop taunted, fishing for any kind of a response. 'But perhaps he wasn't as stupid as we think. Perhaps he knew, all along, that Ava Simmons wouldn't give him the time of day. Perhaps he just *wanted people to think he did*!'

'You're mad, you are,' Janice said. 'Now I've got work to do. Suits of armour don't shine themselves, you know.'

As with Meecham before her, Bishop was forced to watch yet another suspect slip blithely away. He felt like slamming his fist on the table, but very wisely resisted the temptation. He glanced at Miss Starling. 'Well?' he snapped grimly.

Jenny dunked some tomatoes into boiling water to soften their skins for peeling. 'I think Danny *is* a particularly stupid person,' Jenny said mildly. 'But Janice is not nearly as stupid as you imagine.'

And with that, Inspector Bishop had to be satisfied.

He looked around, sensed something was missing, thought about it for a moment, then snapped his fingers.

'Where's that helper of yours. She's usually skulking around with a face like a gargoyle.'

'I gave Elsie the day off,' Jenny lied.

The fact was, Elsie had, very uncharacteristically, left her a note saying that she needed the morning off. Jenny had found it on the kitchen table that morning, when she'd come down. The cook hoped that she hadn't done anything stupid, but she rather suspected that she had.

'Hmm,' Bishop said. 'I think I want a word with her. Myers, let's take a walk down to the village.'

LORD AVONSLEIGH HUNG up the phone and looked across at his wife. 'He's agreed to come,' he said quietly. 'Do you think we did the right thing. Asking *him*, I mean?'

Lady Vee stirred a little on the sofa, and began to fiddle absently with the double rope of priceless pearls hanging around her neck. 'Yes, I think so. Miss Starling sort of hinted that he'd be the best man for the job. And I'd be inclined to agree with her.' Her eyes sharpened on her husband. 'Wouldn't you?'

He smiled. 'Yes. You think she's hit the nail right on the head, don't you?'

His wife's face became grim. 'Yes. I think she has. But what do *you* make of it all? You said very little last night.'

'Well, we'll soon find out. He's coming right over. I sent a car for him.'

'He'll be here soon, then,' she acknowledged miserably.

Avonsleigh nodded. 'Cheer up, old girl. It might not happen.'

She glanced at him sharply. 'It already has, George,' she said, then winced an apology. She reached across and took his hand. 'George, if the worst comes to the worst....'

He nodded. 'We'll manage. We Avonsleighs always do.'

For a few moments they were quiet. 'Bishop's back,' he said at last, giving one of his wife's knuckles an absent-minded kiss, and letting go of her hand. 'I saw his car outside.'

'Hmm. Well, he won't interfere. What he doesn't know won't hurt him,' she replied dismissively. 'But we'll have to make sure that *you know who* and our guest don't meet.'

Lord Avonsleigh's lips tightened grimly. 'They won't,' he promised. 'I've already seen to *that*.'

'But be careful, George,' Vivienne Margaret warned. 'Remember what Miss Starling said. It's imperative that we don't act any differently. We don't want to spook our quarry, so to speak.'

His lordship nodded. He glanced at his watch. Soon they would know, one way or the other.

INSPECTOR BISHOP WALKED into the music-room and looked around. He walked over to the piano and tinkled a few notes, then sat down at the stool and played 'Chopsticks' with just a dash of panache. He was at a loose end, and felt like it. Neither Elsie or her mother had been at home, and he had sent Myers to make inquiries round and about the village.

If Danny was the local meat supplier on the QT, they'd have to have an equally quiet little word with him, too. He sighed. He played again, then spun round as somebody clapped behind him.

'Ah, Miss Starling. Oh, and you too, Lady Roberta,' he said, getting clumsily to his feet.

'Hello, Bish,' Roberta said, bouncing into the room and eyeing the piano. 'What *was* that lovely little composition you were playing?' she asked, her eyes twinkling.

Bishop all but blushed.

Jenny took pity on him. 'Isn't Mr Powell-Brooks supposed to be standing in for your governess, Lady Roberta?'

'Oh, Malc will be here in a minute. He's just tidying up the studio. The workmen have put their backs into it at last and have finally finished putting in the larger skylights. There's bags of light now, but sawdust all over the place. It's driving Malc mad. He insists on a spotless studio. Dirt can get into the paints, you know. But I can start without him,' she said, took a seat, and belted out a dramatic piece that shook the window frames. She gave Inspector Bishop an angelic smile.

'While we're here, er, your ladyship, perhaps you can go over that afternoon again,' he murmured, not to be outdone.

'Oh, Bish!' Roberta groaned. 'Not again! I told you over and over. Malc and I got here about half past two.'

'Not a quarter to three?'

'No. Half past two. We began to play some pieces, you know, warming up, waiting for Simm.'

'What pieces? Can you remember?' Bishop asked, but his tone was automatic. Perfunctory. He was not, Jenny suspected, really listening.

'Some Chopin. Some Bach. A bit of Beethoven. You know, usual stuff. Oh yeah, and the Minute Waltz. I remember that because that was when Malc went to see if Simm was anywhere near. It was getting late by then.'

Lady Roberta suddenly became aware that both of them were staring at her in surprise. 'What?' she said. Then again, more angrily, 'What?'

'You said Mr Powell-Brooks never left this room,' Bishop accused her, trying to keep his tone polite. Trying to remember that she was a lady. Literally.

'But he didn't,' Roberta said, and then waved a hand angrily as she realized the mistake she'd made. 'I mean, he only went to the end of the corridor to see if she was anywhere about. He wasn't gone a minute. In fact, Inspector, I know he was gone less than a minute, because of the Minute Waltz, you see,' Roberta said scornfully. 'That's why I forgot about it. I mean, what you *really* wanted to know was if Malc could have killed Simm, and I knew he wouldn't have had time,' she carried on, suddenly finding the need to justify herself. 'So that's all right then, isn't it?' she added, her chin tilting up challengingly.

'That's all right, Lady Roberta, we all forget things

sometimes,' Jenny broke in, stepping between the exasperated policeman and the indignant lady with a calming voice and a sweet smile. 'Why don't you just start at the beginning and go through it minute by minute? Lady Roberta, did Mr Powell-Brooks leave the room more than that one time?' she began, trying to make sense out of Roberta's somewhat garbled reasoning.

'No, he didn't,' Roberta said firmly. 'And I only forgot about that one time he did leave because he was only gone a few seconds.'

'How can you be so sure?' Bishop asked quickly. 'Time can play funny tricks. A long time can seem a short time, and vice versa.'

Roberta stared at him scornfully. 'I know that. But in this case, I know it was only a short time because of the Minute Waltz,' she repeated, her voice rising in obvious exasperation, her expression clearly stating that she thought the inspector a proper dunce.

'Tell us about the waltz, Lady Roberta,' Jenny said calmly, giving the inspector a shut-up-and-listen look.

Bishop shut up and listened.

Roberta put her head to one side, and sucked on the end of a pencil contemplatively. 'It was, I don't know—about three o'clockish,' she began, obviously making an effort to be perfectly accurate. She was in the doghouse, and knew it, and was touchingly anxious to make amends. 'Simm was half an hour late by then. I'd just done some Chopin, I think, when Malc glanced at his watch. He looked a little miffed. He said he wondered where Simm was, and told me to play something different. He asked me to play the Minute Waltz, and said that that was about all I was good for. But he was teasing, you know.' She broke off, glancing at the cook for back up, and Jenny nodded soothingly.

'Yes, I know. What happened then?'

'Well, I started to play it. Malc said he'd just go down the corridor and see if Simm was in the hall or looked like shaking a leg. He went out and came back again a few moments later. He said she wasn't anywhere to be seen. I hadn't even finished playing it. So you see, he can't have been gone that long. He couldn't possibly have killed Simm in that time, could he? So all this fuss is about nothing,' she finished huffily, and, turning her back on both, her spine stiff with antipathy, she began belting out another dramatic piece.

Bishop and Jenny, not wanting to go deaf, left her to it. Bishop walked quickly down the corridor and saw that it took them out into the main hall. He turned the other way and they found themselves in a small, little-used room that led out onto the same terrace as where their lordships and guests had had their tea that fateful day.

'He couldn't have nipped out this way,' he murmured to himself, ignoring the cook's presence. 'They would have seen him.' Quickly he turned back. At the entrance to the music-room he took out his watch, paused, then took off at a brisk trot.

Jenny was at his heels, although she didn't much like brisk trots. She didn't much like brisk anythings—she simply wasn't built for 'brisk'.

But to get to the conservatory, they had to cross the hall, go up some steps, run down a long corridor and then down some steps again. It was almost a square route to the conservatory and, even as they entered, Jenny knew that the minute was almost up.

Nevertheless, Bishop made a stabbing motion, turned and sped back. Back at the music room, panting a little, Bishop checked his watch.

'Well?'

'Two minutes, ten seconds,' he said.

'And that's without the dagger,' she said.

'Eh?'

'The Munjib dagger. It's down off this little hall here.' She indicated the hall to the left of the music-room. The inspector walked a few yards, and stared up at the dagger. They were leaving it *in situ* for the moment, but soon it would have to go on its merry way to the police lock-up.

'Damn. I forgot about that. He'd have to have retrieved the dagger first. Unless he already had it?' he added, his voice rising hopefully.

'He can't have done,' Jenny squashed that hope ruthlessly.

'The Avonsleighs and the colonel were admiring it at three o'clock, remember?'

'Damn. That'll add another few seconds onto the time.'

'And I don't think Ava would have died quite as quickly as you made out,' Jenny said sceptically, copying his quick stabbing movement. 'And if he'd returned with some blood on him, Roberta would have noticed. She has eagle eyes, that one. And don't forget the fact that he must have somehow rigged it all up so that the

Avonsleighs and guests didn't even so much as see him enter the conservatory, let alone kill her.'

Bishop groaned. 'And I thought we were onto something then. But, wait a minute, this Minute Waltz thing: what if Lady Roberta played it too slowly? Made it a three-minute waltz?'

Jenny smiled and shook her head. 'I don't know all that much about music, Inspector, I have to admit, but I think you'll find that the Minute Waltz is taught to young pupils in order to get them used to tempo. If I remember correctly, it is called that because, played right, it is about a minute and a half long. Only a rank amateur would get the timing wrong. Somebody as advanced as Lady Roberta should, by now, have impeccable timing.'

As if to confirm her words, a dramatic and famous piece from Beethoven's Fifth Symphony wafted out of the music-room.

Bishop sighed. 'So Powell-Brooks was gone less than a minute. Nowhere near enough time to kill the governess.'

'No,' Jenny agreed thoughtfully. She looked up at the dagger. 'It's so beautiful,' she said eventually.

'And so close to the music-room,' Bishop added longingly. Then he shrugged and turned away.

He'd do the timing again. Do a bit of exploring. Perhaps there was a short cut to the conservatory. But he was sure there wasn't, and half an hour later, had to admit defeat.

Malcolm Powell-Brooks had had nowhere near enough time to kill Ava during that minute or so.

Yet another dead end.

Jenny, ignoring the inspector's efforts, continued to stare at the dagger for a long, long, time.

FIFTEEN

THAT EVENING, Inspector Bishop tramped wearily into the kitchen. As usual, whenever Inspector Bishop came in, everybody else went out. Dinner had just that minute finished, and Elsie hastily wiped the last plate and stacked it. Janice and Malcolm glanced at each other and grimaced, whilst Meecham and Gayle rapidly pushed away from the table.

They were all used, by now, to the inspector's odd little talks with the cook. But word had filtered down, as it always seemed to, that their employers blessed this arrangement, so nobody mentioned it. At least, not openly.

'Well, I think I'll read a book and have an early night,' Malcolm said, stretching and yawning a little too enthusiastically.

'Ah, and I've got some knitting to do at home,' Elsie said, just as quickly. 'Now that I've bought a new number ten, that is. That knitting needle of mine never did turn up,' she grumbled dourly, reaching for her cardigan.

'Never mind, Elsie,' Janice said, winking at Gayle, who for once, didn't respond. Instead she followed her father quickly out of the door. From there on, it was a mad rush to see who could get out next. Bishop watched the last departing back and smiled grimly. Jenny eyed him sympathetically, and poured fresh boiling water in the teapot.

Outside, the evening sun was beginning to turn golden. She looked out of the narrow windows towards the lowering sun, and sighed, not unhappily. She liked the short, summer nights.

'Here you go, Inspector. A piece of plum cake? I made it this afternoon.' Inspector Bishop did not pass up on the cake, but then, he wasn't expected to. 'No Myers tonight?' Jenny asked, letting one eyebrow rise interrogatively.

'No. I've sent him off to check up some facts with an electrical shop. It seems your kitchen maid and her mother spent the morning buying a new television. Digital whatnots galore, apparently,' Bishop explained, without rancour. He'd gradually found it less and less of a chore to confide in Jenny Starling so that now he did it automatically. And he had to admit, she'd steered him all right in the past.

'Which makes me wonder,' he continued thoughtfully, reaching for the sugar bowl and heaping two teaspoons into his mug, 'how it is that Elsie Bingham can suddenly afford it.'

Jenny smiled and sat down. She gave a mighty yawn behind her hand and then settled back. If the inspector wanted to spar, she had no objection to obliging him. 'I imagine her father paid for it,' she said mildly, and gave him a reproving look. 'As if you hadn't already figured that out for yourself.'

Bishop looked a shade abashed, then shrugged. 'Blackmail?' He said the one word tonelessly.

Jenny frowned. 'I prefer to think of it in a rather more charitable light, Inspector. More a case of belated child maintenance, I think.'

Bishop conceded the point. He had no sympathies with a man who got a woman pregnant and then abandoned her and his own child. 'Serve him right,' he agreed heavily, then frowned. 'I wouldn't have thought our Basil was the type to stand for it though,' he added, voicing something that had been puzzling him all afternoon, ever since Myers had reported on the delivery van and television set.

'No,' Jenny agreed with him thoughtfully. 'I'm worried about Elsie.'

Bishop chewed on some cake, his taste buds going down on bended knees to thank him. 'It's especially odd since we don't know what she's blackmailing him *about* exactly,' he aired his thoughts out loud. 'I mean, what is she holding over him? We don't believe Basil killed his own daughter. Do we?' he asked sharply. When she shook her head, he carried on thoughtfully. 'And if *Elsie* killed Ava, it would give *Basil* the opportunity for blackmail, not the other way round. So how's she wringing the cash out of him?'

Jenny shrugged. She felt as weary as the inspector. And she was anxiously awaiting word from Lord Avonsleigh. 'I don't suppose she is holding anything specific over him,' she said slowly. 'I mean, she wouldn't really need to, would she? When Ava was first murdered, it didn't really affect Basil financially at all. I imagine, if anything, he even attracted a few more clients to that art gallery of his than usual. Some out of genuine sympathy, but more, I expect, out of morbid curiosity. A little risqué glamour wouldn't hurt—I dare say being associated, however tenuously, with the father of a murder victim goes down well in some ghastly social circles. But with Elsie threatening to make a far more sordid scene—go public on her parentage, hint at something dastardly in the house of Simmons—well, risqué glamour is one thing, but ridicule is another. No one wants to risk being made to look foolish—or crooked.'

'Hmm,' Bishop said non-committally, finishing his cake and looking longingly down for another piece. The cook instantly cut him another chunk. She couldn't stand that 'where's all the food gone?' look. It was the one thing guaranteed to cut her to the quick.

'I suppose the gallery would lose a lot of its customers if Basil's reputation as an upper-crust gent took a bashing,' Bishop conceded. 'But I don't think he'll stand for blackmail for long. If I were you, I'd have a word with your Elsie and persuade her that enough's enough.'

Jenny nodded. She'd already made up her mind to do just that.

Bishop stared forlornly at his cake, his appetite temporarily deserting him as his troubles came flooding back. 'I don't mind telling you, Miss Starling, this case has got me tied up in knots.' He pushed his plate away, clearing room on the table and reached for the condiments. He put a salt cellar down in front of him.

'We have the dagger. The blood on it was Ava Simmons's, no doubt. The lab confirmed the stab wound more or less matched the dagger blade in every aspect. It has an usual rounded edge and a sharp point, as we know. So we know Ava was killed with the dagger.' He reached for his cake and put it to his left. 'We have Ava's body in the conservatory. The amount of blood and lack of any traces anywhere else means that she *had* to be killed in the conservatory. But'—he reached for the mustard, salt, Jenny's cup of tea and his own mug—'we have four witnesses, not twenty-five yards away, who saw nothing.'

For a moment, Bishop stood staring at the scene in front of him. 'We know the dagger was clean and blood-stain-free at three-o'clock. At half past, the deed had been done and it was back in its place, bloodied and guilty as sin.' He paused, took a bite of plum cake, and sighed. 'We've eliminated the garden staff, the Avon-sleighs and guests, and the daily women. That leaves the main suspects. You are out,' Bishop said, compli-menting her without thinking about it. 'That leaves the Meechams, who had a tenuous motive but also a tenuous alibi; Janice, who had a motive and a slightly stronger alibi—although she was seen in Ava's room, she was also seen in town at the time of the actual murder; Elsie, who had a motive and a middling alibi. She could *just* have killed Ava, according to our timing.' He paused to sigh, then shook his head. 'Lady Roberta and Malcolm Powell-Brooks both have a very tenuous motive and an all but rock-solid alibi. Unless they were in it together. I'm beginning to think, you know,' Bishop said heavily, 'that our killer is going to get away with it.'

Jenny reached for the teapot and renewed his mug. 'I wouldn't bet on it, Inspector,' she said softly. 'I wouldn't bet on it at all.'

INSPECTOR BISHOP HAD just gone on his weary way home
when Meecham came and informed her that his lordship
would be pleased if she would join him in the breakfast-room. His voice rose on the final two words, since
it was now nearly nine o'clock at night.

Jenny let him lead the way, knowing how much
the butler needed to feel that his position wasn't being
usurped. Once at their destination, George thanked him
gravely and sincerely, further bolstering Meecham's
fragile ego, and he retired looking a little happier with
himself and the world in general. From a shadowy corner, a man moved and came into the light.

'Hello, Mr Grover,' Jenny said quietly, then glanced
at Lord Avonsleigh who nodded to a nest of chairs by
a blazing fire and made sure Anthony Grover had the
one nearest the flames. Even in summer, the thick castle
walls retained their chill, making fires a year-round ne-
cessity. The rest of them grouped around the old man.

The cook caught Lady Vee's eye. In the firelight,
she looked older than usual, her eyes deeply shadowed.
Jenny glanced again at his lordship. 'My lord?' she said
quietly, and he sighed deeply, but nodded.

'You were right, Miss Starling,' he said heavily.
'Quite right.' For a moment, nobody spoke. Jenny stared
into the hypnotic flames, her teeth worrying her lower
lip. Then she sighed. She glanced at Anthony.

'There's no mistake?' she asked softly, but already
knew the answer.

Anthony Grover shook his head. 'No. I was most
thorough.'

'How many?' Jenny asked.

'Five, that I've found so far. But I imagine there'll be more,' Anthony said. Avonsleigh had explained much of what had been going on, and Anthony had been only too eager to help. Anything to get justice for Ava.

Jenny imagined there would be more too. 'I see,' she said flatly. Although she was being proved right, she felt no satisfaction.

Lady Vee stirred. 'Miss Starling, have you, er, found out yet how it was done?' she asked hopefully, and Jenny sighed.

'Not yet, no. It's maddening,' she went on, 'since I know that somebody, somewhere, has said something vitally important. But I just can't think what.'

Avonsleigh shook his head. 'Vee and I have been going over it all day. We just can't see how it could have been done. Knowing who did it, you'd think we'd be able to figure it out. It is *so* frustrating, as you say,' he finished, giving the fire a ferocious prod with the poker. Some sparks flew out, and the English setter, who'd sprawled out on the hearthrug, gave a sudden yip and jumped up, manically shaking off an ember that was singeing his fur. He gave his master a baleful look, heaved a massive sigh, and promptly re-sprawled himself.

From beneath Anthony's chair, Henry began to crawl towards the dog. The glow from the fire bounced off his dark-brown shell, turning it a deep blood red.

Blood red. Jenny stared at the tortoise, her gaze transfixed. Because, suddenly, she *knew*. She remembered Lady Roberta, swinging her legs as she chatted on, her young voice carefree and happy. She remembered Elsie's missing knitting needle. She remembered a jar of red paint. And she remembered the dagger.

Her mouth fell open. 'Good grief,' she said. For a moment, she could think of nothing else to say, her mind was so stunned. 'The dagger. It was the dagger all along.'

Vee was sitting ramrod straight in her chair, staring intently at the cook. She knew that look. And although the actual words made no sense, she knew that their time was almost up. She glanced at her husband.

Lord Avonsleigh blinked. 'But we always knew it was the dagger,' he said. Had Miss Starling flipped her lid? But that particular thought had never so much as crossed his wife's mind. Instead, she felt her muscles tense. No matter how painful and scandalous it was going to be to them personally, she and George had discussed this at length. Ava Simmons had to have justice. And now it was coming.

As she looked into Miss Starling's glittering eyes and waited, she knew it was coming. Soon. And her heart ached.

'Miss Starling?' Anthony Grover broke the silence, his voice puzzled and slightly worried.

'Hmm?' Jenny started and stared blankly at Anthony. Then she shook her head. 'Oh, I'm so sorry, Mr Grover,' she murmured solicitously. 'We shouldn't really keep you,' she added warmly, and Lady Vee twigged at once. She rose and pulled the bell rope.

'It is getting late, and I know how much we need our beauty sleep these days,' she said, the picture of a concerned hostess. 'Mr Grover, we can't thank you enough for what you've done for us. I can't explain everything now, of course, but....' She caught Miss Starling's eye. 'Perhaps I can call on you sometime soon and then we can have a little chat?'

Meecham arrived at that moment and Anthony Grover rose painfully to his feet, looking a little bemused, but knowing a gracious dismissal when he heard it. 'Thank you, your ladyship. I was glad I could be of service.'

'It's we who should thank you,' Avonsleigh said, holding out his hand. A little flustered, Anthony shook it, and Meecham escorted the old man out. 'The car will take you back, Mr Grover,' his lordship assured him, and gave a glance to Meecham, who nodded.

When they were alone again, Lady Vee glanced at her husband, then at her cook. Without a word, the three returned to their chairs and sat down.

Jenny said again, 'Good grief. It's so simple. I just can't believe how simple it all is.'

His lordship stared at her. He was not quite as quick on the uptake as his wife. 'You mean you know how it was done?' he squeaked, his voice incredulous. To him, the problem had seemed beyond solving.

Jenny nodded. 'Oh yes,' she said artlessly. 'And I can't believe that I didn't think of it before,' she added, beginning to sound angry at herself. 'I'm such a dunce. It was all so *easy*.'

This time it was his lordship's turn. 'Good grief,' he said. 'Was it?'

Jenny nodded. 'And now,' she said coldly, her voice

becoming icy with determination, 'all that's left is to get the proof.'

Lady Vee leaned back in her chair. She felt chilly. 'How are you going to do that?' she asked, squashing—for the moment—her rabid curiosity. 'I mean, murder is hard to prove, isn't it? How are you going to gather enough evidence to convince a jury?' she wondered aloud. She, too, had been beginning to think that the killer of Ava Simmons was going to be too clever for them.

But no longer.

'Basil Simmons is going to get all the evidence I need for me,' Jenny said determinedly, a hard glint in her lovely blue eyes.

'Good grief,' Lady Vee echoed. She reached across, grabbed a cushion and put it behind her back. Then she shuffled in her seat, retrieved the tortoise from behind her back and reached for a more comfortable cushion. This time made of feathers, not of reptile.

'But how was it done?' Avonsleigh demanded, not sure yet whether their total faith in the cook was justified. Besides which, he, too, was feverishly curious.

So Jenny told them how it was done.

When she was finished, they managed it in unison. 'Good grief!'

INSPECTOR BISHOP AWOKE suddenly to the accompaniment of his wife's elbow buried deeply in his ribs, aided and abetted by an awful racket. He winced, half-sat up, and heard his phone ringing. He glanced at his clock, saw that it was 6.30, and groaned.

His wife gave him another nudge with her killer elbow. Bishop grunted, got out of bed, and rubbed his side as he galloped downstairs in an old-fashioned set of pyjamas that would have had Myers howling in mirth. 'Yes?' he all but bellowed into the instrument.

'Inspector?' Jenny Starling's voice came over loud and clear. 'I'm about to prove who killed Ava Simmons. I think, perhaps, the police had better be here, don't you?'

Bishop stared into the phone. He blinked. He opened his mouth, then closed it again.

He hung up without a word.

JENNY WAITED UNTIL Bishop and Myers arrived. They rushed into the kitchen like two dogs called late to dinner, their faces a picture of anticipation and anger. By the stove, Jenny was just starting the sausages.

She looked up and nodded. 'Inspector. Just in time. See that these don't burn, will you?'

Bishop stared at her, then at the pan full of sausages.

'Where are you going?' he yelped as she turned and headed for the door.

'To call Basil Simmons, of course,' she said. 'He's coming over. Didn't I tell you?'

Bishop swore. He swore about once in a blue moon, and Myers, who'd just begun to obligingly turn over a sausage, stopped and stared at him. Hard. 'No, Miss Starling,' Bishop said through gritted teeth, as both his sergeant and the cook gaped at him in amazement, 'you didn't tell me. In fact, you told me nothing of what's been going on,' he ended on a sweet, sweet smile.

'Oh, well. I'd better explain then,' Jenny said crisply. 'But first, let me call Mr Simmons. I want to get it over and done with before any of the others come down.'

Bishop couldn't argue with that. He turned, caught a grin on Myers' face, and swore again. Myers hastily turned back to the sausages. A few minutes later, the cook returned.

'Basil Simmons will be here at nine o'clock. I've arranged with the family to use the sunroom. There's a large tapestry screen there that you can hide behind.'

'And why should I want to hide behind a tapestry screen with Basil Simmons, pray tell?' Bishop gritted.

'You won't,' Jenny said, sounding surprised. 'You and Myers will be behind the screen; Basil Simmons will be in the front of the room.'

'Doing what?' Bishop all but bellowed.

'Proving who killed his daughter, of course,' Jenny said mildly. 'Really, Inspector, there's no need to shout. I'm not deaf.'

Bishop swore again. Most colourfully.

At nine o'clock, Basil Simmons arrived. Meecham, who was operating on strict instructions from his lordship, showed him straight to the sunroom and left.

There, Jenny told the gallery owner exactly what to do and what to say. Bishop and Myers, now brought up to date, stood by in grim silence.

They didn't exactly approve of the plan. It seemed unduly theatrical and amateurish to their official minds. But they had both been forced to admit that it was probably their only chance of catching their killer.

Basil barely glanced at them. But his face, as the cook talked, became blacker and tighter. Finally, he nodded. He, too, was not entirely happy with the plan. But he would go along with it.

At 9.15 exactly, the two policemen retired behind the screen. Jenny also retired, with gratitude, but to her kitchen.

She hated scenes. She loved her kitchen. Once in the sanctuary of the massive room, she began to cook. She was in the mood for it. For lunch, she would make egg croquettes followed by a bread and cheese pudding. Perhaps a fruit compote too. Busily, she began gathering the ingredients. She never looked at her watch, and she kept her mind firmly away from what was going on upstairs.

The kitchen, for once, was deserted. Lord Avonsleigh had arranged to keep everybody—save one—busy.

Jenny had just taken some stale bread from the larder and was beginning to grate it when the door opened. Myers stood at the top of the steps and beckoned her. His face was beatific.

Sighing, Jenny reluctantly left the kitchen and followed him across the hall. Outside, in the ancient quad, was a police car. And just being bundled inside, heavily handcuffed and looking both terrified and furious, was Malcolm Powell-Brooks.

SIXTEEN

THE HALL CLOCK struck two as Jenny and a very happy Bishop and Myers climbed the stairs, following Meecham to Avonsleigh's sitting room. It was a sun-filled room, with heavy oak panelling and large, comfortable leather-buttoned armchairs. He and his wife rose as the trio walked in, Meecham standing to one side and closing the door after them. He was already reverting to the archetypal butler—all cool reserve and calm complacency.

He was not the only one. With the dramatic events of that morning over and the removal of Malcolm Powell-Brooks complete, the whole castle seemed to bask in a lighter atmosphere. The sun seemed to shine a little stronger. The maids seemed to hum a little louder. The dog snored a little happier.

Lord Avonsleigh rose and offered his hand in congratulations to Bishop, who very nearly blushed. Lady Vee winked at Miss Starling and nodded to the small coffee table. On it, rested the little fairy cakes and butter-cream butterfly cakes that she'd baked less than an hour ago.

'Tea, gentlemen?' she prompted, and they all took seats grouped loosely around the laden table.

'So, everything went well at the police station?' his lordship asked by way of openers, and Bishop nodded.

'Powell-Brooks has been charged with the murder of Ava Simmons, my lord,' he confirmed happily. 'He's already talking to his lawyer now.'

'No chance of him getting off, I suppose?'

'No, my lord,' Bishop said firmly. 'We overheard everything said in the sunroom between Basil Simmons and our Malcolm, and Myers here took it all down in shorthand. And, of course, we have it on tape, although whether that will be allowed in as evidence, I'm not sure. Lawyers can be tricky. But then there's the testimony of Anthony Grover, and any other art experts you care to bring in. No, he's not getting away with anything.'

'You're on the trail of my missing paintings, I hope?' Avonsleigh said, and the Inspector nodded.

'We are, your lordship, and I hope we'll locate them for you. But some, I think, are probably lost forever,' he warned, wanting to prepare him for the worst. 'Those sold to unscrupulous private collectors—well, I don't think they'll ever come to light again. But I'm sure we'll track down enough to put the final nail in Mr Powell-Brooks's coffin. It was very clever, my lord, the way you worked out what the swine was up to.'

Avonsleigh coughed behind his hand. 'You're praising the wrong person, I'm afraid, Inspector. It was Miss Starling who worked it all out.'

The inspector paused in the act of lifting his delicate teacup to his lips. The Spode china looked like a child's toy in his massive hands, and Vee felt a fair bit of relief when he carefully returned it to its saucer. The inspector looked at Jenny. Then at his sergeant. Then back to the cook. He sighed.

'All right, Miss Starling,' he said heavily. 'I have to admit it, I'm dying to know how you figured it all out.'

'Yes, so am I,' added Lady Vee eagerly. 'Oh, I know you told us who and why and how, but you never really explained how you came to, well—*know* it all.'

Jenny blushed. 'Well, it was just a simple matter of thinking things through, that's all,' she said, looking and sounding acutely embarrassed.

'Now it's no good being modest,' his lordship cajoled, sounding hearty and jolly and determined. 'Spill the beans, as Roberta would say. We want to hear every last bit of it.'

'In the minutest detail,' his wife added, leaning forward eagerly on her seat. All four, in fact, were leaning forward, their expressions avid, and Jenny sighed heavily.

'Very well. Let's see. Where do I start? Well, we might as well begin with motives, I suppose,' she said, settling back in her chair and marshalling her thoughts into order.

'As you know, at first, there didn't seem to be *any* motives at all. Ava was dead and nobody, as far as we could tell, would want her so. And then, all in a rush, or so it seemed, everybody suddenly had a reason for wanting her gone. I discovered Elsie was really Ava's half-sister, and must have felt resentful of Ava's status. Meecham and Gayle had been cheated out of their farm by Basil Simmons. Janice's boyfriend was making a big play for Ava. Even Roberta....' There Jenny paused, aware that she might be about to step into treacherous terrain.

But her employees both smiled. 'Go on, Miss Starling, do,' Lady Vee urged her. 'We won't be offended. We're much too intrigued to take umbrage, I assure you.'

'Yes, well,' Jenny coughed. 'Even Lady Roberta had reason to resent her governess. Ava was concerned about the relationship between her charge and Malcolm Powell-Brooks, as she had every right to be, as it turned out. Malcolm set out to learn everything he could about Lady Roberta's character. In fact, he relied on it. But that comes later. Where was I?'

Jenny pulled the wings off the butterfly cake on her plate and chewed thoughtfully, unaware that everyone else in the room was straining at the bit, willing her on.

'Malcolm's motive, or so it seemed, was that Ava was jealous of his art degree from Ruskin and was trying to make trouble, get him fired, that sort of thing,' she mused slowly.

'Yes, yes, so everyone had a motive,' Bishop butted in, trying to hurry her along. He was dying to know how an amateur had solved one of the most puzzling cases of his career, and Myers gave him a sympathetic look. He, too, was eager to listen and to learn.

'Yes, but none of the motives seemed, well, really *appropriate*,' Jenny said, groping for words. 'I mean, just think about it,' she urged them all. 'Meecham and Gayle had worked here, quite happily, for years. And it was Basil Simmons, not Ava Simmons, who had caused their ill-fortune. Is it likely, I had to ask myself, that they would kill Ava over *that*?'

She made no mention of The Lady Beade School. Meecham's secret was safe with her.

'Hmm, I see what you mean,' Lord Avonsleigh said. 'It would have been a bit over the top.'

'The same went for Janice,' Jenny continued. 'Granted, no girl likes to see her boyfriend make a play for another woman, but Janice is young and pretty and has had many young lads interested in her in the past, and will doubtless have many more buzzing around her in the future. She already has a new boyfriend now, in fact. Barry, I believe, his name is.' Again, she made no mention of the parlour maid's little game with the brooch. 'So was it feasible, I asked myself, that Janice would be so rife with jealousy that she would kill over it?'

'Of course not,' Lady Vee said. 'Oh, dear,' she added, 'how easy it all is with hindsight, and with someone to tell you what to think,' she added, giving Miss Starling a glowing look. 'What about Roberta and that dreadful man?'

'Well, again, your ladyship,' Jenny smiled back, 'it was all much of the same thing. You yourself told me that you'd had a word with Powell-Brooks and was assured that he wasn't taking Lady Roberta's infatuation seriously. And that Ava seemed to accept your reassurances. So why would he feel threatened enough to kill her? No. Everybody *seemed* to have a motive. But, really, they didn't add up to much. Which meant that there must be another motive. One I hadn't seen yet. So, I had to resort to the three mainstays.'

'Mainstays?' his lordship echoed blankly.

'Money, love and revenge,' Inspector Bishop explained.

'Exactly,' Jenny said. 'But there seemed little hope of finding a motive so well hidden that nobody had even suspected it. But, gradually, piece by piece, tiny clues presented themselves. Some were so general and out in the open that I almost missed them. Malcolm's insistence that Lady Roberta have the best of everything for instance. The best canvasses, the best paints, the finest studio. At first I assumed it was because of who Lady Roberta was, and because Avonsleigh's reputation as a repository of fine art needed to be maintained. But, of course, when you put that aside, the fact remained that Malcolm, a fine art expert, had access to the best of everything himself. And was surrounded by some of the finest paintings in the world. Plus plenty of free time. Nobody interrupted him in the studio when Ava was taking Lady Roberta for her lessons. And with so many paintings in the castle, who would notice if one of them were not in its proper place for a short time? All he had to do was go into a little-used room and take a painting to his studio. Who would notice, or even comment? And what did that all add up to?' she asked, raising an eyebrow.

'An art forger's paradise,' Myers supplied, his eyes glittering.

'Yes. And that brought us back to motive. Money. Lots and lots of money. Malcolm was ideally placed to copy the great masters, replace the original with his own copy, and sell on the masterpiece to private collectors. He was making himself a fortune. No wonder he was resentful of Ava Simmons's interference. If he lost his job here, he lost access to all the paintings. The expensive paints. The old canvasses. That wonderfully equipped studio, with its brand-new skylights that he'd just had installed. Oh, yes, he was a clever man all right. He saw at once that nobody at Avonsleigh was sufficiently interested in art to notice or care what he got up to. Er, no disrespect intended, your lordship,' Jenny added quickly, nodding to George.

He waved a hand. 'You're quite right, Miss Starling,' he agreed, without rancour. 'I respect Avonsleigh's history, of course. Some of my ancestors have been the greatest collectors of art the world has ever known. My great-grandfather was an acknowledged world expert on those French chaps. But I myself never had any leanings that way. I was quite content to keep the tradition up, mind. Have Roberta taught art and keep a resident tutor on staff. What a joke on us that turned out to be,' he added, a shade bitterly. 'I wouldn't have known a Joshua Reynolds from a…from a…Picasso.'

'Oh, I think you might, dear,' his wife said, a twinkle in her eye. 'But I quite get your point, Miss Starling. We all are total dunces about art. But what I don't understand is, how he expected to fool all the others. We do, as you know, play host to several tours of art-lovers every year. Surely they would spot a fake at once?'

Jenny nodded. 'Oh yes. But didn't his lordship say that it was Malcolm who told you when paintings needed cleaning? If you think back, I think you'll find that several paintings needed "cleaning" just before a tour was due to arrive. Those paintings being his own fakes, of course. With such a huge collection, who would miss some? Besides, artworks do have to be cleaned. If anyone mentioned a blank space, and was told it was being cleaned, no art expert in the world would be suspicious. And after they'd gone, he'd just put the fakes back up again.'

'Clever sod,' Myers said bluntly, and received a swift kick in the shins from his superior. Myers coloured. 'Oh, I do beg your pardon, your ladyship,' he said to Lady Vee, and pulled at his tie, which suddenly felt much too tight.

'Oh, you're quite right,' she replied, totally unfazed. 'He *was a clever sod.*'

'But it must have put a crimp on him when Basil Simmons's daughter was appointed governess to Lady Roberta,' Bishop said thoughtfully, and Jenny nodded.

'Exactly. Not only was Ava concerned about the way he could manipulate Lady Roberta, she was an art buff herself. She must have learned a lot from that father of hers.' Jenny just managed to stop herself from calling Basil Simmons something very uncomplimentary indeed. 'And don't forget, you don't need to have a degree from the Ruskin to be knowledgeable. Her mentor, Anthony Grover, was an art teacher himself. Ava grew up with art. She studied it intensely. And it wouldn't have taken her long to put two and two together. No, as soon as she began to suspect, Malcolm Powell-Brooks knew he was going to have to get rid of her.'

'So you think she'd already spotted the fakes?' his lordship said.

Jenny nodded. 'Yes. I'm sure she did. The very first morning I arrived, I saw Ava mid-way on the stairs, and she was studying a painting, very thoroughly. I didn't think anything of it at the time, of course,' she added, her voice losing some life. 'If only I'd had my eyes and ears more open.'

'Miss Starling, you mustn't,' Vee said sharply, making the three men, who hadn't yet caught on, look at her blankly. 'There was no way you could have known what that rotter was up to. You'd only been here a day or two before Ava was actually killed. We'd all been around Malcolm Powell-Brooks for months, and none of us suspected a thing. You simply must not start thinking that you could have prevented it. Evil men kill, and more often than not, there's not a damned thing we can do about it.'

'Oh, quite,' his lordship said, looking as appalled as his wife. 'None of this can be laid at your door, Miss Starling. Nobody here thinks you could have saved poor Ava.'

Bishop and Myers quickly added their own reassurances. Jenny sighed, not much comforted.

'Besides, without you,' Vee continued, 'that dreadful man would have got away with it. And nobody should get away with murder.'

'Quite,' her husband agreed. Then paused. 'Er, about the murder…?'

Jenny nodded. 'Oh yes. The murder itself.'

'Ah,' Bishop said, his massive frame beginning to

quiver, like a hunting dog about to be let off the leash. *Now they were getting to it.*

'That was the hardest part of all,' she continued. 'I mean, it all seemed so impossible, didn't it? The dagger was on the wall, clean and innocent at three o'clock when the family and the colonel and his lady passed it. Then, half an hour later, it was covered in Ava's blood and Ava herself was dead in the conservatory. And four people, who sat not many yards away and should have seen it all happen, actually saw nothing at all.'

'So how did he do it?' Bishop all but yelped. He had listened only hours ago to a man confess to murder, but he still didn't know how it had been done. 'We do need to have all the information soon, Miss Starling,' he pointed out in as reasonable a tone as he could manage. 'The DPP is most anxious to know as well,' he added sarcastically.

Avonsleigh shot him a reproving look, but Jenny missed it, so deep in thought was she.

'Oh, the murder itself was so simple it defied description,' Jenny eventually said, making all four of them want to shake her.

'Simple?' As head of the household, ostensibly, Avonsleigh took the lead. 'I would have thought it was anything but,' he huffed.

Jenny smiled. 'Ah, but that's what we were all supposed to think, my lord. But it wasn't complicated at all. It was easy. Even though a large part of Malcolm's plan went wrong, it was still easy.'

'What went wrong?' Bishop asked, momentarily distracted.

'Why, the family having tea on the terrace, instead of in the sunroom, of course,' she said, surprised that they should ask.

Lady Vee blinked. 'I don't get it,' she said. 'Why should that worry him?'

Jenny sighed. 'The day before, everybody thought that the tea would be held in the sunroom, remember? It had been unseasonably cold for June, and nobody expected you'd eat al fresco. Then, the day of the murder, it turned really sunny and warm, and you decided to have tea on the terrace.'

'That's right, we did. But I still don't see....'

'The only one who didn't know of the change of plan was Malcolm Powell-Brooks,' Jenny ploughed on. 'Meecham knew, since he had to deliver the tray. Janice, Elsie, Gayle and I all knew. Only Malcolm didn't know because, as a tutor, and not a server, presenter or maker of food, he had no reason to be told.'

'But what does that *matter*!' Bishop all but shouted, making everyone in the room jump.

But Avonsleigh understood how the man felt. He too was all at sea.

'Don't you get it?' Jenny asked, looking around at them with wide eyes. 'Malcolm was expecting you to be in the sunroom. Why else do you think he chose the conservatory in which to kill Ava? It was well out of the way of everything, nobody had any business being in there except the gardeners, whom he knew were all working on the pond. It was the perfect place to commit murder. Nobody would accidentally stumble on her body there. Nobody would interrupt him in the deed. There would be nobody to see him do it.'

'But we did,' her ladyship said, then stopped, confused.

'No, wait a minute, we didn't. Of course we didn't. But we *should have*.'

'Exactly,' Jenny said, her voice rich with satisfaction. 'You should have seen the murder, because you were on the terrace. Not in the sunroom.'

'Hang on a minute,' his lordship said, becoming more and more confused. 'What does having tea on the terrace, instead of in the sunroom, have to do with anything at all?'

'That's what I'd like to know,' Bishop growled.

Jenny sighed. Really, they were being so dense! 'Because, the effect of having tea on the terrace meant that you should have seen the murder, but *didn't*! That caused us all so much trouble. *Why didn't you see the murder*?' Everybody stared at her for a long, long, second.

'Because it wasn't committed in the conservatory?' her ladyship offered tentatively at last.

'No, your ladyship,' Jenny said patiently. 'It was committed in the conservatory all right, just *not between three and half past.*'

Again, everyone stared at her.

'But the dagger,' Bishop said, his voice faint.

'Oh yes. The dagger,' Jenny said. 'How that had me fooled,' she admitted softly.

'Look, I've had enough of this,' Lord Avonsleigh said, getting quite heated. 'Just assume, Miss Starling, that we're all duffers. As thick as two short planks and all that. Just tell us, simply, step by step, how the man killed that poor girl.'

Vee shot her husband a loving look. So did Bishop and Myers.

Jenny stared at them, utterly defeated. 'But I just did,' she wailed.

'No, Miss Starling,' Vee said gently. 'You didn't. We're nowhere near as clever as you. Just do as his lordship asked, please.'

Jenny, nonplussed but willing, shrugged. 'Very well. At some time between half past two and three o'clock, Malcolm lured Ava into the conservatory and killed her. He then found Lady Roberta and together they went into the music-room. There they stayed until Meecham found them and told them about the killing.'

'But the dagger,' Bishop said again, feeling a shudder of *déjà vu* flicker up his spine. 'The dagger was clean at three o'clock.'

'But he didn't kill her with the dagger,' Jenny said patiently. 'He killed her with Elsie's knitting needle.'

'Eh?' Avonsleigh said, feeling a bit like Alice, who'd just stepped into the opening of the rabbit hole. 'Knitting needle?'

Jenny blinked. 'Elsie had lost a knitting needle. I learned she was always losing things but, I wonder now if Malcolm just stole little things from her to set up a pattern, so that nobody would think twice about it when she complained that her knitting needle was missing. I wouldn't put it past him.'

'But the medical examiner said it was the dagger,'

Bishop insisted, not letting himself get sidetracked. 'The blood on the dagger definitely belonged to Miss Simmons.'

'The medical examiner,' Jenny corrected him, 'said that Ava was killed by an oddly shaped, rounded-edged instrument with a very sharp point, consistent with the Munjib dagger,' Jenny corrected him. 'But a knitting needle has a long thin, rounded edge. And honed at the tip, it too, would have a very sharp point.'

Vee leaned back in her chair slowly. 'So he stole the knitting needle, sharpened it, and killed Ava at a quarter to three in the conservatory. Then what?'

'Then he went to the music-room. Roberta confirms he didn't leave for less than a minute. She said he was acting just like usual, fingering a small jar of red paint, teasing her just like always. It was the red paint that put me on to it all, of course,' she continued. 'Not that he didn't always have paint in those pockets of his. That was not unusual. But Malcolm had run out of *red* paint the day before—or was it the same day?—that Ava was killed. Lady Roberta had used tons of it on a sunset painting she'd been doing. I myself heard Malcolm ask Janice if she would get him some more when she went in to Bicester. So, if he'd run out of red paint, what was he doing fingering a jar of it in the music-room? The answer, of course, was that he wasn't.'

'You mean Roberta lied?' his lordship asked aghast.

'No, my lord,' Jenny said quickly. 'She didn't lie. She just didn't know what she'd seen. She assumed a little jar of red liquid in Malcolm's hands would be paint. But it wasn't.'

Vee felt her stomach turn queasily, but she had to ask. 'So what was it?'

'It was blood,' Jenny confirmed her worst fears. 'Ava's blood. He'd collected it from her wound after killing her. Janice told me that she'd seen Malcolm cleaning out one of his glass jars very thoroughly, even using bleach, or whatever, and rinsing it out over and over again at the sink. At the time I thought it was because the jar had contained oil paint. But in reality, he just wanted to make sure that the jar was completely spotless, so that no traces of water colour, paint, turps or whatever, would end up in the blood sample he intended to collect from his victim. Later on, after the murder, I saw him rinsing out some other glass jars in a quite a haphazard way, so I knew he was not, by nature, a particularly meticulous man.'

'But why did he collect the blood in the first place?' Bishop asked.

'To put on the dagger of course,' Jenny said, 'during the Minute Waltz. Lady Roberta was sure he was gone from the music-room for not much more than a minute, as he in fact was. But you were with me, Inspector, when we talked to her. The hall with the dagger was less than a few yards away. You yourself proved that he didn't have time to kill Ava. But, by then, Ava was already dead. What he *did* have time to do, was take down the dagger, pour Ava's blood over it, put it back on the wall and return to the music-room. He knew Roberta would never give him an alibi if she thought he could have killed Ava. But if he could prove he was only gone for such a short time, then he was in the clear. Which is why he manipulated Lady Roberta into playing the Minute Waltz in the first place. It was perfect. Except, of course, the family was having tea on the terrace, and not in the sunroom, as he'd thought. So you never saw the murder. *Because it had already been committed.* If you had been in the sunroom, as he planned, nobody would have questioned it. Ava was dead. The dagger was clean at three o'clock, dirty at three-thirty. Ergo, Ava was killed during that time. Except that you all saw for yourself that she couldn't possibly have been killed between three and three-thirty in the conservatory, because you'd have seen it happen. Apart from that, Malcolm had the perfect alibi. Roberta was the perfect witness. It was all so easy. But he must have had a nasty time when he learned that you and your guests had been on the terrace the whole time.'

Vee stared at her aghast. 'Then all that time we were having tea, the poor girl was lying in the conservatory—dead?'

'Yes.'

Inspector Bishop slumped back in his chair. 'Well I'll be blowed,' he said. And winced as Myers kicked his shin. 'Beg your pardon, your ladyship,' he mumbled.

Lady Vee leaned back in her own chair, ignoring his apology. 'It *was* easy, wasn't it?' she said in wonderment.

Jenny nodded. 'All that I needed to do then was to prove it. That was easy enough. All I had to do was get Basil Simmons to confront Malcolm. Tell him that his daughter had confided her suspicions to him, and demand to be let in on the action. And in this case, Basil

Simmons's rather, shall we say, rough and ready reputation in the art world, came in handy. Malcolm could
well believe that Basil wanted in on the money. So he
agreed. And in agreeing, he admitted his own part in
the art fraud, and, by association, the murder of Ava
Simmons.'

'We did better than that,' Bishop put in jubilantly.
'Basil Simmons actually got Powell-Brooks to admit
to the killing,' he told them, grinning a happy grin that
would have made the Cheshire cat go green-eyed with
jealousy. 'And me and Myers here heard it all.'

There was a discreet tap on the door. Meecham
walked in, his face wreathed in smiles. 'Er, there's a
visitor to see you, My Lord,' he said, and stood theatrically to one side.

They all rose as a young man walked into the room.
He was tall, lean and big-nosed, an obvious, younger
version of his father. By his side was a very lean, very
beautiful, very elegant young woman.

'Richard!' Lady Vee yelled, launching herself to her
feet, opening her arms wide and engulfing the young
man in a big bear hug.

Bishop and Myers began to sidle out. Their job was
done.

'Mother!' Richard, heir to Avonsleigh, stood back
and shook hands with his beaming father.

'My boy,' Lord Avonsleigh said happily. 'We weren't
expecting you for weeks yet!'

Meecham beamed. The two policemen had already
disappeared. Jenny began to sidle to the door. She had

dinner to prepare. Pigeon and pheasant pie. Oxtail soup for starters, she thought. She was in a meaty mood.

'Well, I couldn't wait any longer to introduce you to my bride. I know you must be a bit disappointed, me marrying over in America and everything, but'—the young man drew forward his blushing bride—'I just knew you'd love her when you met her.'

Vee met the American woman's eyes and smiled. 'Hello, m'dear.'

'Your ladyship,' the new bride said, her accent, thankfully, quite mild, and not at all the drawling tone Lady Vee had come to expect from watching so many American films on the television.

Cynthia Beatrice, in fact, came from Boston, her ladyship would learn later, not Hollywood.

'Oh, please, call me Vee,' Vivienne Margaret said. 'Well, this is quite a surprise. And a wonderful one.' She caught sight of Miss Starling, sidling to the door, and smiled. 'It's been quite a day, I can tell you. Richard, we have a lot of catching up to do. But first, you must be famished,' she said.

Jenny's ears pricked up almost as high as those of the English setter, who was watching the proceedings with a swishing of his plumy tail.

'Oh, we are,' Lord Richard said.

'Miss Starling,' her ladyship said. 'Some soup and sandwiches I think.'

'I have some oxtail soup already made,' Jenny said happily, making for the door.

Now that the murder was solved, the castle was happy again. The heir and his bride had returned from overseas, and the cook could see only happy days stretching ahead of her. Long, happy days of cooking the great British dishes, in a great British castle, for a real lord and lady. Bliss!

'Oh, not for me,' Cynthia said quickly. 'I don't eat meat.'

'Don't eat meat?' George said, his voice an appalled whisper.

Vee's jaw dropped.

'Oh no,' Cynthia said. 'I'm a vegan.'

'Vegan?' Lady Vee echoed faintly. 'But I thought you were an American?'

The newlyweds both laughed. 'She is, Mother,' Richard said. 'But she's a strict vegetarian, too.'

'A vegetarian!' Jenny yelped, unable to restrain herself. Everyone turned to stare at her. Lady Vee met the cook's outraged face, and her own eyes began to fill with tears. Her lower lip began to quiver pathetically.

Jenny drew herself up to her immense height, her back becoming ramrod straight. A vegetarian!

Lady Vee, seeing this, quite rightly, as a further sign of impending disaster, found her chin was beginning to wobble alarmingly. Bravely, she fought back the urge to burst into tears.

Lord Avonsleigh, for once as quick on the uptake as his wife, saw his spotted dick and custard fade into the distance, and his eyes, too, began to water.

'Yes,' Lord Richard said, his voice quiet but firm. 'Do you have a problem with that, Miss er...?' He had no idea who this stranger was, but he didn't appreciate her look of horror one little bit. Any hint that his darling wife wasn't as perfect as she so obviously was, was most definitely not going to be contemplated.

Jenny said nothing. She was, at that moment, and for the first time in her life, utterly speechless.

Instead, she looked forlornly at Lady Vee.

Lady Vee looked forlornly and helplessly back.

And before either one could disgrace themselves, Jenny turned and quickly walked out.

EPILOGUE

MEECHAM KNOCKED ON the door to the breakfast-room and came in gingerly. He took a quick look around, but Lord Richard and the American bombshell were nowhere in sight.

Avonsleigh looked up from his paper. Lady Vee, who was standing at the window looking out over the west garden and the village, turned to glance at him, a mournful look on her face.

Meecham coughed. 'The cook has just left, m'lady,' he said miserably. His lordship ducked back quickly behind his paper, lest the butler see the renewed tears in his eyes. Meecham glanced at the breakfast plates. Segments of fruit and raw vegetables still lined the plates.

Meecham remembered back to the good old days of last week, when he'd collected empty plates with only smears of egg, marred only by bacon rind and the odd bit of tomato skin. He sighed and picked up the plates, then stared down at an untouched carrot stick and felt woefully inadequate. He coughed. 'Er, we in the kitchen, that is, the staff, have taken of late, to…er…buying some cereal, your ladyship. In a packet,' he added, not sure whether they were au fait with corn flakes. When his lordship looked at him, he coughed again. 'I was wondering, my lord, if you and her ladyship might, er, possibly benefit from a dish of corn flakes of a morning. That is, if….'

'Meecham, you're a godsend,' Vee boomed from her window, cutting across his nervous embarrassment. 'By all means, sneak us a bowl of corn flakes whenever you can. But make sure *he* doesn't catch you.'

Meecham bowed. *He* was the new chef Richard's American bride had all but forced down their throat. An American, like herself, he was one of those new guru-type of individuals that had sprung up lately, preaching healthy living and to curse all animal fats.

'No, my lady,' Meecham said, with feeling. 'I'll make sure the, er, chef, doesn't catch me.'

There was something almost rabidly fanatic about the new chef. The way he chopped vegetables was really alarming. And all the new kinds of vegetables he was bringing into the kitchen…well, Meecham didn't like the look of them at all. Foreign things they were. Things you never even heard of, let alone wanted to eat. Ugli fruit for instance. Ugli it looked and ugli it tasted, in his opinion.

He sighed woefully. For a week now he'd been forced to watch Miss Starling showing the new chef around, standing aside as he cooked, her lips pulled into a thin, grim line. She'd looked fit to blow a gasket, but she never had. Instead, she'd always managed to cook around the chef, coming up with something good for the staff. And with Meecham's help and some expert planning, they had even managed to slip the family the odd steak and kidney pie or fish-and-chip supper when the American bombshell and Lord Richard were dining out.

But no more. Miss Starling had given her notice on the day of Lord Richard's arrival, and for a week they'd been dreading the day she'd go. And now the evil moment was upon them. Even the odd clandestine steak and kidney pie was now but a pipe dream.

Meecham heaved another sigh, collected the plates and left.

Lord Avonsleigh waited until he was gone, then got up and joined his wife at the window. 'I must say, I do think it's a bit thick,' he complained. 'I never thought Miss Starling was the sort to abandon us in the trenches.'

Lady Vee snorted. 'Nor is she, George, nor is she. But you simply can't ask a cook of her calibre to restrict herself to vegetables. It, well, it's demeaning. It's insulting. It's like asking Sir Christopher Wren to restrict himself to designing garden sheds. Or asking one of those orchestra johnnies to play a violin with one string missing. It just isn't cricket.'

Her husband nodded glumly. As ever, his darling wife was right. 'She might have stayed on and cooked my puddings, at least,' he mumbled, unwilling to let it rest.

'With what, dearest?' Vee snorted. 'I've looked up what "vegan" means. It means not only is meat off limits, but anything else that comes from a bird or animal. So poor Miss Starling wouldn't be able to use eggs, so there goes any kind of sponge pudding. She mustn't use milk, so bang go our tapioca and rice puddings. Unless it was fruit, fruit, fruit, it would never get past that creature Richard hired.'

George went pale. 'I've been thinking, old girl. That new chef of ours. Do you think we might, well, bump him off?'

'Bump him off?' she repeated, giving her husband a fond look. 'Well we might, George. And with Miss Starling gone, we'd probably get away with it too. But'—she patted his hand fondly—'I don't think it's quite on, do you? After all, the chap's a foreigner. You can't go about potting foreigners. They do take on so.'

He sighed. 'I suppose so. So what do we do?'

Vee smiled. 'We wait, George. Richard is the next Lord Avonsleigh, and his wife the Lady, so we must be careful not to alienate them. For the moment, the American bombshell—that's what the staff are calling her behind her back, you know—is having it all her own way, because Richard is still so young and head-over-heels in love with her. But the honeymoon stage doesn't last long, and the rose-tinted glasses will come off, sooner or later, you mark my words. And don't forget, George dear, Richard is our son. He'll soon start to crave a nice bit of rump steak. He'll start dreaming of roast lamb and mint sauce. And then....'

'Then we'll get Miss Starling back,' his lordship said firmly.

'Exactly. I'll word an advertisement that only Miss Starling will recognize and understand, and put it in *The Times*. You'll see. Despite having to always cook *one* vegetarian dish for the bomb...er, Beatrice, she'll come back to us.'

His lordship sighed. He wondered if the colonel had a cook that knew how to make real spotted dick with custard. He'd have to get himself invited over....

'Oh, look, there she is,' she said, craning her neck. Below them, solitary rucksack in hand, Jenny walked briskly across the lawn. Her bright cherry-red van was currently in the village, lodged in the local mechanic's front garden, getting itself a good overhaul.

'She's headed for the short cut to the village,' his lordship muttered, his voice thick with emotion. 'I do hope she hasn't felt *too* put out about all this,' he added worryingly.

Vee watched the cook put down her rucksack and suddenly veer off to the left, heading unerringly towards Seth's carefully fenced off vegetable plot.

She blinked. 'I rather think, George, that she has felt a little bit bitter,' she said mildly, her tone wavering on the verge of laughter. 'Look who she's just picked up.'

His lordship, a trifle far-sighted, leaned forward and peered. 'Well, it looks like—good gad, it is. She's got Henry! Vee, our cook's kidnapping our tortoise!' he yelled, aghast.

Vee bit her lip, laughter gurgling at the back of her throat. 'I don't think that's what she has in mind dear. Watch.'

He watched.

As she neared the carefully protected rows of beans, carrots, cabbages, lettuces, beetroot and radishes, the large, shapely cook stopped and looked around furtively. Then she quickly hoisted the tortoise over the chicken-wire fence and set him down firmly in the nearest row of lettuces.

* * * * *